VISION

Vision
ISBN: 978-1-60920-008-4
Printed in the United States of America
©2010 by Ann Aschauer
All rights reserved

Cover and interior design by Ajoyin Publishing, Inc.

Library of Congress Cataloging-in-Publication Data

API
Ajoyin Publishing, Inc.
P.O. 342
Three Rivers, MI 49093
www.ajoyin.com

Please direct your inquiries to admin@ajoyin.com

VISION

by

Ann Aschauer

Ajoyin Publishing, Inc.
PO Box 342
Three Rivers, MI 49093
1.888.273.4JOY
www.ajoyin.com

DEDICATION

To all the readers who loved Counselor and hounded me about the sequel, sorry this book was so long in coming! Thanks for your patience.

To Pam, thanks for all your help and encouragement in the aspects of publishing where I was clueless. Sherry, thanks for sharing your creativity in designing such beautiful covers.

To my zany cousins, for making my childhood so hilarious and giving me endless ideas for stories. Thanks for the great memories, and for continuing to be zany and fun as we all race towards our "golden years."

To my husband and children, in-laws, and now grandchild! Marty, Joanna, Ben, Kelly, Sean, Rachel, and Caroline, thanks for making my life so full! I love you!

Most of all, thank You, Lord Jesus, for all of the above, and for Your amazing love.

Disclaimer

While the events described in this novel are based on real experiences and people, it would be a mistake to make any assumptions as to specifics. The storyline is designed to convey truths, not precise facts in detail.

Unless otherwise indicated, Bible quotations are taken from the Holy Bible, New International Version, Copyright 1973, 1978, 1984 by the International Bible Society. Used by permission of Zondervan Publishing House. The "NIV" and "New International Version" trademarks are registered in the United States Patent and Trademark Office by the International Bible Society.

INTRODUCTION

The man stood there, gazing at Liz through thick glasses and smiling fondly, as though he were her best friend. And she did feel as though she should know his name, but the memory was so dim that it seemed like a distant dream. She was somehow familiar with the crooked way he stood, the cane that supported him, and the slightly contorted fingers curled around the handle. Inexplicably, her heart gave a leap.

"I ... I know you," she murmured, staring at him. The young man seemed to understand her befuddlement, and although the thickness of his lenses appeared to distort his eyes, she sensed acceptance from him.

Yes! His name was ... It began with a "J"... Her mind was struggling; she had known once who he was. If she could just remember ...

"You're ... you're ..." Suddenly the deep scars on the hands caught her eye, and the answer came to her, but the thought seemed almost blasphemous. Finally, she dared to say it out loud.

"You're Jesus."

He smiled at her with a gentle nod.

"But ..." again she struggled to understand. "If you're Jesus ... aren't You supposed to be ... perfect?" She cringed at the thought of questioning the Lord's perfection, but she couldn't ignore the brace on the scrawny leg and the fingers curled almost into a fist. To her relief, the affection on her Friend's face didn't change.

"I am perfect," He answered, not proudly but merely stating fact. He paused, casually glancing down at the imperfections, then looked back into her eyes and added, "but My body isn't."

It was then that Liz saw behind the heavy lenses the tears glistening in His eyes.

The harsh ringing of the phone startled Liz out of her dream. She fumbled for the receiver and mumbled hoarsely, "Hello?"

"Liz! I'm sorry, did I wake you up?" Sarah's chipper voice was in stark contrast to her groggy friend's. "I wanted to catch you before you left for the day."

"Uh, yeah, that's OK, Sarah." Liz tried to focus her eyes on the clock. "—Oh wow, I overslept, didn't I?"

"Yeah, I'd say. You OK?"

"Yeah. I was having a dream..."

"Really? What was it?!" Sarah asked eagerly. She loved hearing about Liz's dreams.

"It was about, let's see... There was ... I saw ..." Liz's mind was in a fog. She sighed. "Shoot, I can't remember."

"Oh well. Lord, if it's important, please help her remember it." (Sarah had a habit of praying in the middle of conversations, even on the phone, since she was firmly convinced that Jesus was always right there with her.) "I just called to tell you Michael got called in to work tonight, so we're moving the Bible study to my place."

"Oh. OK ..." Liz wasn't feeling very chatty. "So, I'll see ya tonight."

"OK, see ya later!"

Liz tried to drag herself out of bed, but the adrenalin-charged, end-of-the-year activities, the late night studying, and the final exams were taking their toll. Instead, she found herself lingering, letting her mind go where it wanted, which this morning was a replaying of recent events.

After four years at the University of Illinois's Krannert Center for the Performing Arts, Liz's dream of playing a major role had finally come true through their production of *The Sound of Music*. For over a month she had acted, sung, danced, and lived as Liesl Von Trapp, sixteen, (going on seventeen) where she had known every word to say, every note to sing, every step to dance. And, after she had fallen for an attentive understudy named Aaron, it had seemed like a fairy tale, headed for "happily ever after."

But with the end of the play had come reality, which unlike a script, can be both unpredictable and complicated. Since Aaron did not share her newfound faith in Christ, Liz had been forced to choose between Jesus and him.

Liz pondered again the significance of that choice. She still found it hard to believe that she—timid, emotionally needy Liz—had had the strength to choose Jesus over a doting friend she could see, hear, and touch. But then, she never could have made such a decision without His help. And the fact that He had come through for her convinced her all the more that she had made the right choice, even if it meant that both of her lifelong dreams—playing a major role and having a "significant other"—seemed to have come and gone like a summer shower.

For a moment she relived the pain she had felt after such a sacrifice, for the more intensely she could feel that pain, the more she would also be able to relive the delight of what had unexpectedly transpired next. She was glad that this morning for once she had a few extra minutes to indulge in such a luxury.

God has a way of surprising people, Liz had learned, especially when they have obeyed with seemingly nothing to gain. And, as quickly as Aaron had been taken out of Liz's life, Sean had been brought into it, as their long-time friendship had suddenly blossomed into something more. It was sudden for Liz, anyway; as she had learned, Sean had cared for her from Day One. Liz basked in the memory of that revelation, relishing every detail, every word that had been said, and the same warm and wonderful feelings swept over her once more.

"Thank You, Jesus," she sighed. "You've been so good to me."

She would like to have lain there for an hour or two more, but just then the bells of Altgeld Hall chimed, reminding Liz that while memories are all well and good, time marches on, and focusing on the future was a little more essential at the moment, especially for a certain pair of college seniors.

After graduation Sean would be heading for his home town of Chicago. He had already accepted a position on staff at a large church there, where he planned to head up a new drama ministry. Liz was invited to come for a short visit, or for a long one, or indefinitely. Liz was a writer with a keen sense of the dramatic, and Sean was hoping she would write at least some of their material, having recognized her talents in some of the theater classes they had attended.

Of course, the fact that he had been in love with Liz for four years had probably had something to do with the invitation as well.

While Liz loved the thought of writing for a drama ministry, the sudden change in career plans made her a bit uneasy. She had always lived the kind of life where everything was carefully thought out years in advance, so this turn of events had nudged her considerably out of her comfort zone.

Now it was the week of exams, and soon, for what it was worth, Liz would be the proud recipient of a University of Illinois diploma. Staring into the mirror at the pale, freckled face, framed with tangled, cascading auburn curls, she found it hard to believe that soon, with her degree in acting, she would have an impressive new title.

"Elizabeth Danfield, Bachelor of Fine Arts," she murmured.

"Whoever *that* is," she added with a sigh.

Between the concrete walls of Krannert Center for the Performing Arts, sound always carried more than one would think. At times this condition was unfortunate.

"I heard she went off the religious deep end," a young, know-it-all voice reverberated. "Go figure."

"They made such a cute couple!" said another sadly.

"Poor Aaron!" chimed in a third with exaggerated compassion.

The three stopped abruptly as Liz walked into the green room. There was an awkward silence, and everyone present was pretty sure that Liz had heard at least the tail end of the conversation. Their exchanged glances asked one another just how much of it she had heard.

Liz's face felt hot, but she greeted them as though nothing were awry, and the students exchanged trite comments about the upcoming exams. Liz fumbled with some change and impulsively purchased a candy bar from the vending machine in order to justify her presence in the briefest way possible. She then left quickly, as though she were late for an appointment, but chiefly to escape the gaggle of gossips before the tears spilled over. As she left, she could hear the conversation continuing in more hushed tones; the only words she heard clearly were "Sean" and "rebound." Outside the green room she angrily flung the candy bar in the trash and hurried for the exit.

She was in such a rush to leave that she nearly collided with the student coming in.

"Oh, I'm sorry!" she stammered, then found she was looking into the face of the one friend she felt she had left in the theater department.

"Liz!" Sean laughed. Then seeing the tears, he stopped short. "Are you OK?" She hesitated for a moment, and he said decisively, "We're going for a walk." He put his arm around her, did an about face, and began walking her out.

"Weren't you on your way somewhere?" she protested.

"It wasn't important," he assured her.

They walked in silence for a moment. Then Sean asked gently, "Why are you hurting?"

Liz didn't want to hide anything from him, but neither did she want him to hurt the way she did. So she stared ahead and answered evasively, "I wish certain people would mind their own business." For a moment she wanted to take back the words, fearing that Sean might think she was saying *he* was the one who should mind his own business. But he knew her well enough to know exactly what she meant.

"You've heard them talking about us?" By the look on her face he knew he had hit the nail on the head. "Yeah, me too."

"You have?" Liz was surprised—and a little annoyed—that he was taking it so calmly.

"Yeah. So what?" he smiled at her and shrugged his shoulders.

"Well, ... so ... I don't know," she laughed sheepishly. "I just heard them saying stuff that was... well … not real complimentary."

"And their opinion is important because...?"

Liz was stumped, so she just exhaled deeply.

"It just bothered me, that's all." She was encouraged to hear herself say "bothered" in the past tense.

"Why did it bother you?" Sean asked.

Again, "I don't know." Liz smiled back at her friend. "I guess 'why?' and 'so what?' are questions I should ask myself more often."

"There ya go!" said Sean with a wink and a "thumbs up." Liz had been encouraged by Sean's little trade mark so many times in the past four years, and she was still realizing just how special he was to her. She gave him a wink and thumbs-up back, then hugged him. His friendship was worth more than all the others put together.

"Liz, you and I are in the minority." He produced a rag from his pocket. "Your ring needs polishing again," he added parenthetically. Liz looked at the silver ring she had worn since junior high summer camp, which she had never been in the habit of cleaning. Polishing it had become one of the little things Sean did for her as a sign of his affection. Slipping it off, she handed it to him, and he rubbed vigorously at the tarnish as they continued to walk.

"If you're gonna follow Jesus, you just gotta get used to being misunderstood. Remember what He told you that time in your dream?"

Liz had shared with Sean her dream in which she had met Jesus—or "J," as she had called Him—at least what she had remembered of it. She knew what part Sean was thinking of now.

"I don't have many friends, Liz, and you won't, either," J had warned her. At the time, gazing into His eyes, it hadn't seemed to matter what anyone else thought.

"That's OK," she had confidently responded. *"You're all I need."*

But running up against the shallowness and cruelty of people, especially unexpectedly, had reminded her how badly others' words could hurt.

And yet now, being with Sean, Liz knew deep down that the opinions of others weren't the most important things in life. When he handed back her ring, nicely polished, she sensed a certain profoundness in the gesture; he had cleared up her tarnished thinking as well.

"Yeah, I guess the sooner I get used to it, the happier I'll be," she said, slipping the ring back on. "Besides, I've got *quality* friends. That's what matters." As they walked on in silence for a few moments, something still felt unresolved.

"I just don't want *you* to believe our relationship is a 'rebound' thing," she said. "That *is* important to me."

Sean stopped short. He turned to her, grasped her shoulders, and stated emphatically, "Our relationship is an answer to prayer! They don't understand *us*, because they don't understand *prayer*." He looked thoughtful, then added, "In fact, come to think of it, they don't know God, so they don't understand much of anything."

Liz thought about that, and suddenly she pitied the green room gossips.

"So I guess I just need a thicker hide," she said.

"That would be helpful," Sean agreed. "A thick hide—but a tender heart—don't ever lose that. It's tricky, but Jesus can help you have both."

"Yeah. Right now I just want to graduate and get out of here."

Sean put his arm around her and gave her a squeeze. "It won't be long. Meanwhile, are you gonna be able to come to Bible study tonight?"

Liz thought of the group of friends that had become like family to her, and she couldn't help smiling. "Yeah. I wouldn't miss it."

"'There are different kinds of gifts, but the same Spirit,'" Sean read. " 'There are different kinds of service, but the same Lord. There are different kinds of working, but the same God works all of them in all men.'[1]"

"Thanks, Sean," said Dana. "We can see that in this room, can't we?" She looked around at the assortment of students that crowded the little living room, some in jeans, one in a loose-fitting dress, and one still in his uniform, having hurried over from his job at Armedo's.

"There's Sarah, the gifted therapist—our 'angel of mercy' with the healing touch. And Ray makes us laugh." A few people snickered at the very mention of his name, and the clueless look of "who, me?" on the young man's face brought a chuckle to the rest of the group.

"And Dana's a born teacher," added another student appreciatively. Dana smiled modestly.

And what am I? Liz wondered. *A singer? Actress?—Writer? Dreamer?*

The group went on reading the list of spiritual gifts: wisdom, knowledge, faith, healing, miracles, prophecy, discernment, tongues, and interpretation of tongues. It all sounded so foreign to Liz. For one thing, she had never heard of "speaking in tongues" and had no desire to do it, whatever it was. She thought it sounded weird and nasty. But what was read next gave her a sudden sense of déjà vu.

"'The body is a unit, though it is made up of many parts; and though all its parts are many, they form one body. So it is with Christ,'² " Ray read.

"Thanks, Ray," said Dana, looking up from the page at the group. "Have you ever felt 'out of it' or inferior, because you weren't just like Christy Christian or Holy Harry?"

"*OH* yeah!" sang out a refreshingly honest freshman who sat cross-legged on the floor. Liz smiled at him; *his* gift was making others feel normal.

"Do you ever envy other people's gifts?" Dana asked. Liz thought of the nearly four years of envying the girls whose names appeared on the cast lists, who received roses in the dressing room, who stood in the spotlight and took extra curtain calls. She couldn't help remembering, once she had landed a part, how quickly the time had flown and the show was over. She also couldn't help noticing that none of the spiritual gifts listed in the Bible had anything in particular to do with show business. *Maybe it's time for a reality check,* she thought. *Priorities.* They seemed to have been changing ever since she had come to know ... Him.

"Comparing yourself to other people can be a trap in two ways," Dana went on. "First of all, you may be tempted to disqualify yourself from the Body of Christ because you're different from the Christians you see around you. But you're different for a *reason!*" she stressed.

"For instance, can you imagine a body that's made up entirely of eyes? Or ears? Or *feet?*"

"P.U.!" Ray thought out loud.

"'Now the body is not made up of *one* part but *many*,'" Sarah continued the reading. "'If the foot should say, 'because I am not a hand, I do not belong to the body,' it would not for that reason cease to be part of the body. And if the ear should say, 'because I am not an eye, I do not belong to the body,' it would not for that reason cease to be part of the body. If the whole body were an eye, where would the sense of hearing be? If the whole body were an ear, where would the sense of smell be? But in fact God has arranged the parts of the body, every one of them, just as he wanted them to be. If they were all one part, where would the body be? As it is, there are many parts, but one body.[3]'"

There it was again. Déjà vu.

"Thanks, Sarah. Now on the other hand," Dana went on, "if you feel just fine about your gifts, thank you very much, listen to this part: 'The eye cannot say to the hand, "I don't need you!" and the head cannot say to the feet, "I don't need you!"[4] So what's the second danger?"

"Arrogance," said one student.

"Self-sufficiency," said another.

"Exactly! Don't start thinking you're more important than someone else, just because you might get more attention," said Dana. "For all we know, the guy who cleans the toilets in the church might be just as important as the preacher. Only God knows. So, we need to respect one another, *and* ourselves. We need to appreciate one another's gifts *and* be happy with our own." Dana closed her Bible and looked up.

"When Michael asked me to lead the Bible study tonight, I wanted to share this passage with you, because it has meant so much to me. One of the biggest things God did for me was to help me love myself. When I was growing up, I felt so inferior to certain people around me. I wanted the confidence I saw in the kids that looked down their noses at me, but that wouldn't have been good, either. Thankfully, God got a hold of me and showed me He made me unique, for a reason. Now I can know that I *am* special—but so is everybody else!" she added with a grin.

She read on: "'On the contrary, those parts of the body that seem to be weaker are indispensable'[5] …" Liz was feeling a strange connection with what was being said, but she didn't know why. She just had the feeling that what she was hearing was extremely important for her to grasp.

"… 'But God has combined the members of the body and has given greater honor to the parts that lacked it, so that there should be no division in the body, but that its parts should have equal concern for each other. If one part suffers, every part suffers with it; if one part is honored, every part rejoices with it.' "[6]

"Did you know that if someone lost their big toe, they wouldn't be able to walk properly?" Sarah asked. (Being a future physical therapist, she found all this talk about coordination of the body to be right up her alley.) "But we don't think of a toe as that important. But just think of how much pain we can be in from something as small as a tooth."

"Or a torn cuticle!" added Tiffany, who worked part-time as a manicurist.

"Exactly!" said Dana. "So, people who may not seem that useful to us may be a lot more important than we think."

An image of a student with multiple handicaps flashed across Liz's mind, and she felt as though she were grasping for something just out of reach.

Dana read on: "'Now you are the body of Christ, and each one of you is a part of it.' "[7]

Liz's head snapped up. *The body of Christ!* Suddenly the whole dream came back to her. She nudged Sarah. "I just remembered what I dreamt this morning!" she whispered.

"I think I know what Liz's gift is," Sarah announced. Liz blushed as she looked at Sarah inquisitively. "She's a visionary! A creative thinker. She has dreams, imagination, insights ..."

Vision! The face with the thick glasses—the face badly in need of vision—appeared to her more clearly than ever. Suddenly she found herself "thinking out loud."

"Would it be fair to say that Jesus is perfect, but His body isn't?" she asked.

The statement seemed to take Dana by surprise. There was a pause.

"I never thought of it exactly that way before, but now that I think of it, I guess it's true. Wow…That's a pretty profound observation, Liz."

"If we're the body of Christ, you might even say that He's ... handicapped," Liz suggested. A couple of people started to laugh, but stopped abruptly as the truth of the statement sank in. "I guess there's trouble when one part isn't doing his (or her) job, or tries to do someone else's job."

"That's true," said Dana thoughtfully. "So… We need to pray that we'll know where we fit in, what our gifts are, and what the *Lord* wants us to do."

"Not what *we* think would be neat," Liz added, not necessarily to the group.

There was a murmur of agreement, and Liz went on following the train of thought.

"I always thought the life for me was on stage, in the spotlight, seen by a lot of people. Strange, since I'm generally so scared of people... It seemed like a glamorous life, but I'm beginning to think that's not my calling at all."

What was it Sarah had told her about cerebral palsy? That the problem wasn't in the hands or feet, but in the connections in the brain. If the limbs weren't hearing what the brain was saying, they wouldn't know what to do.

"When you think about it," she went on, "the most vital parts of the body—like the brain and the heart—aren't seen at all. But they affect everything around them. If any other part gets disconnected from the invisible organs, the whole body starts falling apart."

"Wow," said Brad, an athlete who had his eye on the major leagues. "I'm gonna have to think about this some more."

After the others had left, as Liz was helping Sarah clean up, she told her about the dream that had come back to her during the Bible study.

"Wow," said Sarah. "Pretty relevant to what we were talking about tonight."

"The thing is," said Liz, "When He told me His body wasn't perfect, it felt as though He was asking me to do something about it. But what can I do?"

"Well, for starters, you can be whatever part He wants *you* to be."

"Which is ... ?"

"Well, think about the gifts He's given you. That should at least give you a clue." Liz thought a moment about some of the things that had been said that night.

"Sarah, what did you mean by 'visionary'?" she asked. Sarah paused.

"Oh, that? Just that you see some things the rest of us don't. Certain things about the Lord—before you even knew it was Him—possibilities, maybe even the will of God. Are you thinking what I'm thinking?"

"That He wants me to be an eye or something?"

"Well, the Bible does say, 'Where there is no vision, the people perish.'[8] With your dreams and your writing ability, maybe He wants you to help bring more vision to the body of Christ."

"That's an exciting thought," said Liz, almost afraid to start dreaming about it.

"Yeah. When you get one of those profound insights, just write it down. Of course," she teased, "a writer isn't often in the spotlight taking a bow."

"Who cares?" said Liz, feeling liberated by just how much she meant it. "I just want to do what Jesus wants me to."

Sarah put down the dishrag and turned to her.

"Y'know, Liz, I believe you really do."

The chimes from the nearby church announced that it was 11:00. The girls hadn't realized how late it was getting, but although Liz fretted about how early she was going to have to get up the next day for her last class in costume design, she knew the Bible study had been a badly needed break and a time to regain perspective.

When they got to the door, Liz turned and smiled at her friend, and as the two hugged each other, Sarah whispered to Liz, "Remember, *write it down!*"

Liz's sister Elaine once said, "Everybody should have at least one crazy uncle," meaning of course that a family would be dull indeed if everyone in it were one hundred percent normal. (Never mind the fact that the term "normal" is debatable.)

Uncle Jack seemed to fit the bill—or at least the Uncle Jack that seemed dedicated to the proposition that insanity isn't a frame of mind, it's a way of life.

Lest there be any misunderstanding, the Owen Jackson that was married to Aunt Ellen, a true Southern Lady, always played the Southern Gentleman when in her presence. He clearly could be refined when the situation called for refinement; his manners were impeccable. He was as much at ease in a tuxedo as he was in his overalls. He had an immense vocabulary which rolled off his tongue in a rich, deep voice, with a Southern accent that gave the impression of a pre-Civil War plantation owner. Indeed, that was almost what he resembled in the large family portrait that hung over the fireplace in their Tennessee home. The painting showed Owen Jackson standing erect and Aunt Ellen seated beside him. They were surrounded by their sons, Douglas and Bobby, and their daughter Amanda. The tiny Yorkshire terrier, "Vivie," (named after Vivian Leigh) sat in Aunt Ellen's lap, and even their bloodhound, Jefferson Davis, showed a dignity that no one ever saw in real life. Such was the image Owen Washington Jackson had among "polite society."

But with his children, nieces, and nephews, he was "Daddy" and "Uncle Jack," and seemingly a completely different person. Liz could never tell whether her cousins got their zaniness from their father or if Uncle Jack got it from them, but they appeared to feed off each other, and harebrained schemes just seemed to materialize out of the blue. To Uncle Jack the world was teeming with adventures waiting to be had, and he and his sons (and even Amanda, when Aunt Ellen permitted) were off to find the adventures, or else create some of their own. Liz didn't know much about the family's life in their home on the outskirts of Nashville, but she had observed them in the summertime in northern Michigan when all the cousins on her mother's side could spend time together.

The Jackson's summer home was more like a mansion by the lake, and the atmosphere was like a trip back in time. In the foyer an antique telephone hung on the wall, chimes and clapper on top, crank at the side, and a dial that had been installed to "modernize it" decades before. Although they could afford any "toys" they wanted, Liz's aunt and uncle staunchly refused to stock "the cottage" with video games, a VCR, or TV. An antiquated record player from past generations was the chief source of electronic entertainment. (Since it was only used on inclement days, the scratchy quality of the vinyl records from the past blended with the rain on the roof and was hardly noticed.) On sunny days the Jackson family spent their time exploring the woods, climbing the dunes, and enjoying virtually every water sport known to man—and some unknown ones that Uncle Jack just invented on the spot, such as being dragged behind the sailboat on a windy day wearing a mask and snorkel.

During the summer Liz was able to observe first-hand the eccentricity of the family: the way Aunt Ellen used the good china in an attempt to make the dinner table elegant, even though the dinner guests were frequently still in swimsuits and towels; the way the boys would have a scratchy record of *Madame Butterfly* playing in the living room and get into a wrestling match in an argument over whether opera could be considered true classical music, during which Uncle Jack sat in front of the immense stone fireplace pensively smoking his pipe. (Aunt Ellen had implored him to quit smoking the thing, but after a week of the alternative—cigars—she had begged with equal fervency that he take back his pipe. Liz thought the pipe looked and smelled much better, anyway.) When he was smoking in the big easy chair and staring into the fire, Uncle Jack had a classic look of sophistication, but the children knew that, ten-to-one, he was dreaming up tomorrow's excursion into borderline insanity—the "Uncle Jack Zone."

One day her uncle had taken the children into the woods to a secret place he had discovered long ago, where the wreck of a small plane sat rusting, filled inexplicably with *Life* magazines from the 1930s and 40s. Liz cringed to think how they had taken armloads of the publication back to the house with them without asking anyone's permission, to look at and marvel over on the next rainy day. (*Why couldn't history class at school be this much fun?*) No one ever claimed them or had Uncle Jack arrested, so she had figured the owners must be long gone.

There was the night of Uncle Jack's birthday, when halfway through Aunt Ellen's gourmet dinner Jefferson Davis began baying wildly outside the kitchen door. Uncle Jack and the boys sprang from the table to check out the commotion. Amanda and Liz were torn between going with them and politely staying at the table with the grownups. Soon there was shouting and scrambling for Uncle Jack's hunting rifle, and when the boys came running back through the house with Uncle Jack in his safari hat from Zimbabwe, followed by a yipping Vivie, the girls apologetically left the table to join in the excitement. Aunt Ellen merely sighed and whispered a prayer.

The cause of all the ruckus turned out to be an enormously fat raccoon that had been living on the family's garbage all summer. Perched in the tree over the trash cans, it stared down at the noisy mob with glowing eyes. Bobby, the youngest cousin—who was screaming "Kill it!" with ecstatic glee one moment and the next moment was wailing with belated compassion, "You killed it!"—came running in to tell Aunt Ellen that Uncle Jack had bagged a 'coon, and could she stuff it and put it over the mantle so their house could be a "*real* cabin"? Aunt Ellen replied that she most certainly would not, and he could just tell Uncle Jack to take the creature out back, where Emma, her "help," could do with it what she pleased. (This might have explained the unidentified gourmet meals that showed up on the table the next few nights, and the strict diets that every member of the family suddenly decided to take up.)

Cousin Amanda got married early in the summer that Liz was fourteen. This event was a miracle of sorts, since most boys who were ever interested in Amanda usually ended up more fascinated by her father and brothers and their antics. Amanda had often had to choose between joining them and being a perpetual tomboy or submitting to Aunt Ellen's attempts to turn her into a lady. In the end she wound up being a little of both, and apparently Tommy Matthews thought she was perfect that way.

Although Liz had seen two distinct sides of Uncle Jack most of her life, that summer she saw yet another facet of him. As with most fathers-of-the-brides, he was a bit overwhelmed by the experience of giving away his "li'l girl" to another man, however wonderful that man might be. Liz noticed a redness in his eyes as he walked his daughter down the aisle and a catch in his voice when announcing, "Her mother and Ah do," when asked, "Who giveth this woman…?"

His poise and humor never faltered, though. At the reception he rose with his glass of champagne and banged his spoon on his water glass for attention.

"Unaccustomed as Ah am to public speakin'," his deep voice boomed, and the audience chuckled. (Uncle Jack's speeches were famous.) "Ah do have a few words to say to y'all. But Ah'll keep it like mah li'l girl… short and sweet." (*There's that catch in his voice again,* thought Liz, which explained why he was keeping it short.) Uncle Jack paused and took a deep breath, gazing affectionately at his daughter. His eyes again turned uncharacteristically red, and he blinked and looked instead at his new son-in-law. His voice again grew strong as he bellowed out for all to hear:

"Ah wish you joy. Ah wish you peace.

Have lots o' fun, and may the trahb increase!"

Amanda blushed, glasses clinked, and Uncle Jack sat down, coughing and blinking hard.

Later he danced with his daughter, waltzing with both grace and gentleness, as though he had been given a glass doll to hold for a moment. When the groom approached to cut in, the father of the bride turned her over to him with a sweeping, magnanimous gesture, like a king giving away half his kingdom. Then, walking up to his own bride, he took her hand, and with a bow inquired, "Lady Ellen, may Ah have this dance?"

She accepted.

The magic and elegance of that night was exceeded only by the sheer lunacy that followed.

The bride's brothers had slipped out of the ballroom to find the getaway car and to tie multiple tin cans to the bumper, only to be interrupted by their tuxedo-clad father who demanded in his booming voice, "Now what d'y'all think you're doin'?!" The boys meekly stepped aside as their father strode over and took the cans off the bumper with one yank.

"Ya don't tah 'em where everybody can *see* 'em!" he scolded. Then Uncle Jack got down on his hands and knees and reached up under the car, muttering to himself, "…boys don't have the brains God gave a turnip…"

"Tah 'em *here*," he explained. "That way they can't see 'em, and they'll wonder if their muffler's fallin' off."

(The Jackson boys had a lot to learn about "weddin' pranks.")

Later on, Douglas and Bobby, guilt-ridden about the Limburger cheese they had put in the newlyweds' engine, decided that to atone for their sin they would make up a "peace offering" for the happy couple. They took a basket from one of the tables, dumped out the rolls, and filled it with goodies—a box of Fiddle Faddle, their carnation boutonnieres, a copy of the *TV Guide,* two packs of Hubba Bubba, and a GooGoo

Cluster. Uncle Jack threw in a couple of his old cigars when Aunt Ellen wasn't looking and advised the boys to just leave it outside the newlyweds' door.

"Don't you boys knock, y'hear?"

The boys called the hotel desk to see what room the newlyweds occupied, but instead of answering their question, the desk clerk connected them by phone. The guests let it be known in no uncertain terms that they did *not* wish to be disturbed. The boys then went to the desk personally to get the room number. The clerk this time merely told them the number, but as they were headed for the room to leave their peace offering, the clerk then called the newlyweds again to tell them two young gentlemen were on their way up to see them and was again informed that they did *NOT wish to be disturbed!* What followed was a run-in with the hotel security guard, who found it hard to believe a pair of newlyweds would have any use for a *TV Guide*. Uncle Jack was paged by the front desk and went up to claim his boys and come back to the ballroom with some sort of explanation for Aunt Ellen, who demanded to know why half the family had disappeared before the wedding guests had started to leave.

Uncle Jack smoothed everything over, however, kissing her hand and calling her "the belle of the ball," and saying that in the radiance of such a rose, who would miss a few thorns? He sealed the speech with one more dance, while the boys sneaked out back to find out what it was like to smoke a cigar and why Aunt Ellen was so dead-set against it.

Uncle Jack never said outright that it broke his heart giving away his "li'l girl," but he did declare that the rest of the family was going north early that year for a change of scenery. Much to Liz's delight, they invited her to go up with them, since Amanda's room would be available. Since Liz's family planned to go a couple of weeks later, she could join them then. She was glad to be included, since Elaine had gone on a biking trip to Europe with her friends, and the quieter Liz felt that maybe for once she would get to go somewhere without being upstaged by her sister.

The Jacksons picked up Liz in St. Louis and drove caravan-style, since two adults, three children, two dogs, and all their gear for the summer would never have fit into one vehicle. Every hundred miles or so there was a "tradition" they had to keep up, and at each stop they would rearrange the seating so no one would have to put up with Jefferson's slobber, Vivie's yapping, or Uncle Jack's pipe tobacco for the whole trip; that way the nuisances were evenly divided. The cousins played games made up by Uncle Jack, kept in touch with each other with their Mattel walkie-talkies, and fought over the Game Boy until the batteries were worn out anyway. When they had finished the fudge from one of their traditional stops at a tourist trap, they tore the box into pieces that they let Jefferson chew on in order to produce "offensive weapons" that they chucked at the other car, only to be pelted with peanut shells in retaliation. Liz was amazed that Uncle Jack and Aunt Ellen could concentrate on their driving with all this going on, but then she noticed that her aunt was driving with stereo headphones over her ears and a look of serenity on her face. As for Uncle Jack, he was trying to "sing along" with the rapper on the radio and doing a very poor job of it, which merely provided one more source of entertainment for the passengers. Then the boys started making up their own rap, which was equally ridiculous, until Liz's sides ached from laughing.

By the time they arrived at "the cottage," the sun was setting over Lake Michigan, and everyone was hot, sticky, and tired.

The minute they opened the house they noticed what the kids called "that Michigan smell," which was a sort of combination of pine, mothballs, and the slight mustiness of a house that has been closed all winter. It was neither a pleasant nor unpleasant smell, but a unique one that got everyone excited about another summer that had only just begun.

Liz was shown to her room, a small bedroom with a slanted ceiling and a window that overlooked the water. As she unpacked she observed the various keepsakes Amanda had collected from twenty-some summers spent at the lake: a favorite doll, a Petoskey stone Uncle Jack had no doubt helped her polish, a dried flower from the wedding of a friend, and a shoebox full of snapshots. Liz took the liberty of looking through the pictures, many of which were of Amanda and her father—proudly holding the fish one of them had caught in the Bahamas, Uncle Jack's showing ten-year-old Amanda how to hold a baseball bat, and their laughing at a family cookout, their faces smeared with barbecue sauce. One snapshot was of three-year-old Amanda as a flower girl, wearing a long lacy dress, clinging to a basket with one tiny hand and Uncle Jack's hand with the other. Liz was surprised by the twinge of heartache that struck her when she saw it. She felt bad for Uncle Jack, giving up his li'l girl after all those years. Summers would never be quite the same for him.

No sooner had they settled into the cottage than Uncle Jack decided to drown his sorrow in a nautical adventure up the coast of Lake Michigan. The boys of course were ecstatic.

"South Manitou!!!" they yelled, with many a "Yoho!" and other expressions no doubt meant to sound "salty," but with their accents they sounded more like a cross between Jack Sparrow and Forrest Gump.

Aunt Ellen was obviously not in favor of the notion, but she was clearly outnumbered and kept her dignity by refraining from protesting. She merely said, "I hope you boys see to it that your father stays in the boat this time. That yardarm was funny—*once*."

"What d'you mean, 'you boys'? Liz is comin' too! Aren't you, Liz?"

Liz was incredulous. The Jacksons' high seas voyages in their seventeen-foot sailboat were legendary. She had heard so many tall tales around the campfire about their adventures and the sights they had seen that they seemed more like local folklore, but now she was being invited to go along! Again Aunt Ellen sighed with resignation and just said, "Elizabeth, honey, if you want to go, you'd better call your parents and ask them."

"Yeah, call 'em quick and tell 'em we're leavin' tomorrow!" said Douglas.

"*Tomorrow?!*" cried Aunt Ellen. "Douglas, you must be joking. It's out of the question! …Owen?"

But the others were paying no attention to her. While Liz called home, Uncle Jack and the boys tore into the odd-shaped storage closet under the stairs and began pulling out musty sleeping bags, a tent, coils of rope, canteens, a camping stove, and other necessities. Aunt Ellen went into the kitchen to start packing some of the groceries she had just bought and to make another shopping list. A few minutes later she was on her way to pick up some last-minute supplies in "the village."

As Uncle Jack and the kids were piling their gear by the front door, Aunt Ellen came in, looking concerned.

"It might not be a good idea for you to leave tomorrow," she said. "I just heard the marine forecast on the radio, and there's a small craft warning…"

"The Thistle is *not* a 'small craft'!" Uncle Jack declared indignantly.

On the other hand, the Thistle wasn't exactly what one would call a mighty sailing vessel. The boat was at least twenty-five years old and made of wood. The Jackson boys had been in such a hurry to get it into the water that day that they hadn't touched up the paint or varnished the interior. But the hull was sturdy, they guessed. At any rate, it didn't seem to leak, and if it did, there was an empty coffee can for bailing…

Aunt Ellen sighed and counted the life jackets.

To Liz's surprise, her parents had consented to the adventure, since they had every confidence in Uncle Jack and Aunt Ellen's judgment, and besides, in St. Louis they didn't get the marine forecast.

Twelve hours later, a small craf—er, seventeen-foot sailing vessel, loaded down with four sailors, two dogs, and enough gear to equip an Arctic expedition, bobbed on the waves as it motored out onto Lake Michigan. The dim morning light filtered through grey clouds as the boys began hoisting the sails. Ropes tangled and untangled, and a spider or two scurried away as sails that had been packed all winter unfurled in the wind.

The air was cold and fresh-smelling (upwind from the musty sails, anyway) and the waves slapped against the sides of the boat, sending spray into the air. Liz pulled her windbreaker a little tighter as a gust whipped her pigtails around her face. Jefferson Davis stood erect in the bow like a canine figurehead, and even Vivie seemed excited, sitting next to Uncle Jack in her tiny life preserver. (It didn't exactly make her look like a "salty dog," and the boys thought it was ridiculous, but Aunt Ellen had insisted.)

At last the sails billowed, the motor was turned off, and they were on their way. Douglas and Bobby broke out the Hohos, and Uncle Jack lit his pipe. Liz took a deep breath and smiled. She was on an adventure with her favorite uncle, and all was right with the world.

Liz didn't know why she had awakened with all these familiar visions of Uncle Jack running through her memory. She hadn't seen her uncle since the summer before, and then it was not like these distant images of him. He had been thinner, weaker, smaller somehow, and although he had smiled and had that familiar, endearing boyish twinkle in his eyes, he was clearly tired and in some pain. His laughter was less hearty, his speech a little slower, and the atmosphere in the Jackson summer home had been more subdued. The "boys" (now in their twenties) had clowned around as usual, but with slightly less gusto, and Amanda's face had betrayed a sadness Liz had never seen in her before. Jack's li'l girl, now a mother of two, had sat on a log between her husband and her father at the beach fire watching Uncle Jack help her three-year-old put a marshmallow on a stick, and when the family was singing camp songs and Uncle Jack patted her knee, she had laid her head on his shoulder, her eyes glistening in the firelight.

Liz knew Uncle Jack had been diagnosed with cancer, but she had assumed his weakness was the effects of his treatment; surely if anyone could bounce back, Uncle Jack could. After all, another summer was coming. There were woods to be explored, adventures to be had…

But now she knew something she had not known last summer, that there was much more at stake than "adventures," even than life itself. She had known, of course, that death comes to everyone, though like most people her age she avoided thinking about it. But in recent months she was being made aware that not only was death not the end, but also that going to heaven was not a "given." Contrary to popular opinion, being a lovable, adventurous, funny guy wasn't the key; the key was the forgiveness of sins, and there was only one way to obtain that.

Oh Lord, she prayed. *Does Uncle Jack know You?* She thought of his involvement with social and political issues—his "good deeds." Some of them had been done through his church. *But does he really **know** You?*

She thought about the night before, the Bible study, her talk with Sarah, her growing conviction that writing was her calling. She had been thinking about writing poems, articles, stories, maybe even books, and she had wondered, was she good enough to get published?

Now the thought occurred to her that maybe the Lord was asking her to start with something more personal, for a much smaller audience.

A letter? she asked, and something within her cried, *Yes!*

Immediately her mind was bombarded with feelings of misgiving. She hadn't really elaborated about her conversion to her family, who assumed she had always been a Christian, since she had been born into a "Christian" (church-going) family, had gone through confirmation, and was basically a "good girl." They probably also assumed Uncle Jack and Aunt Ellen were Christians because they'd always been a "Christian" (church-going) couple. Liz could imagine the family's reaction if she dared to tell someone so much older and more churched than she was about God and salvation.

Her mind tried to rationalize. Maybe Uncle Jack *was* a Christian. She certainly didn't want to insult him by implying that she thought he wasn't. But was inoffensiveness worth risking eternity?

The answer was obvious. She pulled out a box of stationery and some scratch paper.

Oh Lord, help me, she prayed. Maybe this writing thing wasn't going to be as easy as she had thought.

She scribbled a rough draft on the scratch paper, looked up some Scriptures, made some changes, added a paragraph at the beginning, rewrote an entire section, and set it aside to go to her exam.

At noon she came back and read over the rough draft, and although she made two minor changes, she was surprised at how well it flowed. She felt satisfied that it said what it was supposed to say, and she thanked God for answering her prayer. Glancing at the clock, she got out a piece of stationery and pen and wrote neatly and deliberately:

Dear Uncle Jack,

How have you been? You have been in my thoughts and prayers lately. I was just thinking this morning about all the good times we've had together during our summers in Michigan. Do you remember when we went to South Manitou, when

Vivie fell out of the boat in her little life preserver and Jefferson rescued her? And when Douglas read "The Birds" around the campfire and no one wanted to be the first to go back to the tent because there were all those seagulls all over the beach? Remember when the tent collapsed on Bobby, and he panicked because he'd been dreaming about giant birds and he thought one had him? What a trip! Thanks so much for letting me come along. It's one of those things I'll always remember.

I wanted to write to you and share what's been happening in my life, because it has changed my whole outlook on everything—life, death, and eternity.

If anyone had asked me a year ago if I were a Christian, I probably would have said, "Yeah, I guess so," because I was raised in a church, got confirmed, generally obeyed the Ten Commandments, etc. (I was a "good girl.")

But in the past few months God has been revealing Himself to me in the most unique ways, which I don't have time to go into detail about now. But I've come to know Jesus very personally, as I've never known Him before. He's my Best Friend now, and He's been teaching me a lot, not only about who He is, but about myself as well. I've been learning new things through the Bible study I've been going to and reading the Bible on my own, and I've realized that I've gone through life with some major misconceptions. I want to tell you what I've discovered. (Forgive me if you already know all this.)

As Romans 3:23 says, "All have sinned and fallen short of the glory of God," which is another way of saying "Nobody's perfect." OK, duh. Next point…

"The wages of sin is death, but the gift of God is eternal life through Jesus Christ." (Romans 6:23) I hadn't realized that "death" also refers to spiritual death—that sin makes us unfit for heaven. But we've all sinned in one way or another—What a predicament!

(Actually, this makes sense, because if a person with sin—an imperfect person—entered a perfect heaven, it wouldn't be a perfect place any more, no matter how many good deeds the person had piled up.)

This really upset my concept of a giant scale with "good deeds" on one side and "bad stuff" on the other. It's not a matter of being good but of being perfect, and the only way to achieve that is to somehow have our sins erased. As for you, if it were a matter of good versus bad, your good deeds would have tipped the scales so fast you would have been catapulted into heaven by now!

But we don't get to heaven by tipping the scales, but by having our sin taken away, and the Old Testament says "Without the shedding of blood, there is no *forgiveness of sin." This is why the "Chosen People" (Israel) were always making animal sacrifices—to atone for their sin. But Jesus, who never sinned, allowed Himself to be killed on the cross as the ultimate atonement. (When I understood this, I realized why He's called "the Lamb of God.") Because He died for all of us, anyone who believes in Him can be forgiven and saved from an eternal death. The Bible says, that "to all who received him, to those who believed in his name, he gave the right to become children of God."*

So I'm writing to ask you, do you know Jesus? Have you received Him as your Savior? The way you've lived your life tells me yes, you have a relationship with him, but even if there's one chance in a million that you don't, I don't want to take that chance, not with eternity at stake. I know now after twenty-one years of being a "good girl" that being good isn't enough. We need Jesus.

Maybe you and I have many more years on this earth—I hope so. But I know life is uncertain. I could get hit by a bus when I go to mail this letter. But I know that whether I die today or ten years from now or seventy years from now, I'll spend eternity with God because of what Jesus did for me. I really hope you'll be there, too.

I love you!

Liz

Liz read the letter over, addressed the envelope, put a stamp on it, read the letter again, and prayed, "Please God, don't let him be offended…" then stopped short with the thought, *Priorities!* "…I mean, God, if he doesn't know You, please use this letter to bring him to you before it's too late."

There was still a knot in Liz's stomach, and she added, "and if anyone else in the family is offended, please help me to respond as You would."

She picked up the phone. "Hey Sarah? Would you mind praying with me about something?" She explained the situation, read the letter to her, and then sat in silent agreement as Sarah prayed. It was a much longer prayer than Liz would have said, but every word of it expressed her desire, too. So at the end she just said, "Amen. And Lord, thank You for Sarah!"

Sarah was encouraging. "Well, Liz, you love your uncle, you've obeyed the Lord, you've spoken the truth, and we've bathed it in prayer. Expect the best."

But prepare for the worst, Liz thought.

Uncle Jack was in Liz's prayers much of the next few days. Her active imagination fantasized about answering the phone and hearing his booming voice declare, "Praise the Lawd, Darlin'! Ah'm saved, and mah whole household, too!" At the same time, her insecurity imagined a call from Aunt Ellen saying "How dare you—! As sick as he's been, and you go upsettin' him like this!"

After three days it was apparent that this might be one of those times she wouldn't know the results of her actions or prayers until much later, maybe not in this life. She tried hard to give it to the Lord, but still she checked her voice mail frequently for any word from Nashville.

And she prayed.

When a call finally came, it was not from Nashville, but from St. Louis.

"Liz honey, this is Mom." The voice sounded sad but not shocked; Liz knew before she said it. "Uncle Jack passed away this morning."

"Oh…"

"The funeral's Monday morning in Nashville, so you should get your tickets to fly there Sunday. Aunt Sue and Uncle Walt said we could stay with them Sunday night."

"Yeah… OK, Mom. … How's Aunt Ellen?"

"Holding up pretty well. I don't think it's quite sunk in yet."

"Yeah, I guess not." *(I know the feeling.)* "OK, I'll, uh, make the reservation and let you know the flight and everything." Liz hung up the phone with an empty feeling.

I guess I'll never know, she thought.

The family reunion that took place was pleasant in spite of the circumstances. Liz couldn't remember the last time she had seen so much of the extended family together— aunts, uncles, cousins, (first, second, "once removed???") she hadn't seen in years. Even Elaine had flown in from California to make a rare but brief appearance. *What a shame it takes death to bring us all together,* thought Liz. Talk of Uncle Jack seemed to revolve around funny stories about him, how he had brought joy and laughter to the family. His children were all there, Liz's favorite cousins. They were so much like their father, their informal attitudes and body language contrasting with the elegance of their surroundings. The stately old house, which had been in the family for generations, was dripping with history. An oil painting of an ancient relative (No one ever seemed quite sure who exactly it was.) hung above the sofa, flanked by two ornate sconces. Heirlooms and antiques adorned every corner, and photos old and new were displayed lovingly on shelves and walls, so that one never could feel quite alone at Aunt Ellen and Uncle Jack's. The "boys" lolled about on chairs from various periods, tossing satin pillows at one another, their grief thinly veiled behind the familiar laughter, as if pretending nothing had changed would somehow make it so. Even with all her training in the theater, Liz couldn't quite get into the simulated merriment at the moment; she just felt like hugging "the boys," as Uncle Jack had affectionately called them for the past twenty-some years.

"I remember how Bobby practiced the piano under the tyranny of Great-great Uncle Beauregard," Douglas laughed, nodding toward a portrait of a distinguished-looking gentleman over the baby grand. Liz gave him a questioning look. Bobby explained.

"You know how sometimes you can see the smile, and sometimes you can't?" Liz checked out the portrait.

"Wow, you're right…"

"Well, after I'd been playin' a while, I'd look up at Uncle Beau, and if it looked like he wasn't smilin', I'd figure I'd better practice some more. Sooner or later I'd look up and see him smilin', so I knew it was OK to quit."

"You are so weird!" Liz laughed, throwing a pillow at him; Uncle Beau seemed to be smirking. "So all the time I thought you were such a diligent pianist, it was really your Uncle Beaureg—"

When Aunt Ellen entered the room, she stopped abruptly. Liz's heart went out to her when she saw the dark circles under her eyes and the way her clothes hung loosely on her gaunt frame; she seemed to have aged ten years since Christmas. Still a warm smile and politeness flowed from her so naturally, obviously from a lifetime of training in "southern hospitality." She was a true lady, but a badly hurting lady. As their eyes met, she made her way across the room to Liz.

"Liz darlin', how good to see you!" she smiled through tear-filled eyes. As they embraced, Liz noticed her reluctance to let go. Aunt Ellen then looked into her eyes and said quietly and seriously, "I need to talk to you later."

Hoo-boy, thought Liz. *Am I in trouble?* Her expression must have said as much, for Aunt Ellen squeezed her hands and said, "It's all right, honey. Nothin' bad." She then went to greet Liz's parents.

"I want you to see something," said Aunt Ellen. They were in the master bedroom, and Liz's aunt shut the door against the noise of the growing crowd downstairs. They sat on the huge canopied bed, and Aunt Ellen picked up a box from the bedside table and took out a familiar envelope. Liz's heart jumped at the sight of it. Uncle Jack had received her letter!

Aunt Ellen said, "The mornin' Jack died, he told me he was ready. He had peace with God. He said he was a *real* believer in Jesus. I wasn't sure what he meant by 'real.' Then I found this. Oh darlin' I hope you don't mind my reading' it. It was lovely!" As again tears filled Aunt Ellen's eyes, she glance down at the third page.

And when I got to this part...'Have you received Him as your Savior?' he squeezed my hand and looked into my eyes. He was weak and breathless and could only say one word. But, honey, that one word...was, 'Yes!'" Her face beamed and Liz gave a little gasp of joy.

The two women embraced, and this time both were in no hurry. Together they wept for joy. Finally Aunt Ellen dabbed her eyes with her handkerchief and said between sniffles, "I prayed for years he'd come to the Lord. I thought probably he had, but I was never sure. You know Jack, all fun and games, but he had a hard time talkin' about the real personal things. And I was always reluctant to ask him outright. If he was in a questionable mood, I didn't want to stir up trouble, and when he was in his usual good mood, I didn't want to ruin it!" Her voice began to break. "Oh honey, I don't know how I could have endured losin' him if I didn't know!" Aunt Ellen took Liz's hands in hers and gave them a squeeze. "But now I know. *Bless you* for askin', darlin'!" Something in her eyes twinkled through the sadness.

"Oh, and honey," she added, "welcome to God's family!"

So she knew Him, too! Liz knew now that Aunt Ellen was going to be all right.

Liz had to fly back to Illinois later that very afternoon to prepare for graduation. She regretted not being able to spend more time with Aunt Ellen, "sharing" about their experiences with Jesus. But now that she knew Aunt Ellen knew Him, she was sure they would have a chance some other time, when there weren't so many people around and the circumstances weren't so intense.

As the plane was being boarded, Liz sat by the window, hoping the seat next to her would remain vacant. She had so much to think about and pray about that she didn't want to have to make small talk all the way back to Illinois.

Her unspoken prayer was answered in the affirmative, and as the engines started and two perky flight attendants demonstrated the safety features Liz had seen a hundred times before, her mind was free to ponder what had transpired in the last twenty-four hours.

Her first assignment from God as a writer had gone well, but then Jesus *had* said "My yoke is easy; my burden is light."[1] Still, she knew her endeavors to do God's will wouldn't always go so smoothly and have such a pleasant outcome. Jesus had also said, "In this world you will have trouble."[2] Sarah had jokingly pointed out that scripture with a sarcastic reference to "precious promises."

Well, if God knew her inside and out, (and she had no doubt that He did) He knew what she was and wasn't ready for. How kind of Him to give her such an encouraging start. And His timing had been just right. If she had waited a week to write that letter...or even another day—!

So Uncle Jack was at peace with God, as he probably had been all along, Liz wasn't sure. But she was sure that though the road ahead might be darker for Aunt Ellen, at least she would have the comfort of knowing where Uncle Jack was, and that she would be seeing him again. People say "at least," but as Liz and Aunt Ellen knew, that made all the difference.

And God had used Liz to give her aunt that enormous gift! Ordinarily she wouldn't like the feeling of having been used, but having been used by *Him* gave her a rush of satisfaction.

And a desire to be used more. But as the plane began to taxi down the runway, and Liz looked around at all the people on board, she wondered … *If this plane were to crash, killing everybody, how many of us would be with the Lord, and how many … wouldn't?* The alternative was unthinkable.

Suddenly she saw the selfishness of her desire to sit alone.

Lord, if I'm going to be an eye of sorts in the Body of Christ, help me to see things as You do, and help me to communicate that vision to the rest of Your Body. The prayer was out practically before she knew what she was asking for. Sarah had told her about the Holy Spirit's helping Christians when they don't know what to pray; maybe this was one of those times.

Liz looked down at the buildings that were quickly getting smaller. It occurred to her that every one of them had people living or working there, and that every person down there would spend eternity either with God … or not. It suddenly dawned on her how it must break Jesus' heart to see so many people He died for who were still lost, without hope. After all, He loved them, and knew them as well as He knew her, down to the number of hairs on their heads, the Bible said!

Liz focused on one house. Who lived there? What was life like for them? Did they know Jesus? She saw a car, a tiny speck on the road.

Lord, bless and direct the driver of that car. Show them Your will, and if they don't know You, let them know You love them…

She saw a factory and prayed for the workers there. Her heart felt a stirring.

She saw a school and prayed for the students. Her eyes began to fill with tears.

She saw a hospital and was overwhelmed. She clapped her hand over her mouth for fear a groan would escape. *Oh Lord…* she began, but couldn't go on. She sat in stunned silence as the buildings got smaller and smaller and finally disappeared behind the clouds.

*It **hurts** to see things as You do!*

Then, though no one was sitting next to her, she heard a voice, a voice from the past. It was actually a dream from the past. Like a flashback she heard "J" saying softly but clearly,

"Write me a song."

As the voice on the P.A. system announced that refreshments were being served, Liz stared out at the clouds, deep in thought, until she was interrupted by the attendant taking her drink order.

After getting her drink and pretzels, she pulled her journal from her bag and turned to some blank pages in the back. As quickly as she had her pen ready, words began to come.

Yes! That's what I want to say! It even rhymes! Thank You, Lord! Then … *Hmm… no, that's a better word…*

She jotted down words, she paused, she erased, she jotted some more, and as she wrote, a beautiful melody was taking shape in her mind.

When she got to the end of the last verse, she got "stuck."

"And I wonder, in a world of darkness, how to help them see?"

Hmmm…*"starting with the person sitting next to me"? Too corny!*

Writer's block. Oh well, it'll come later. She sat back and went over the song again and again in her head until the plane landed, fearful that she might lose that gorgeous melody before she had a chance to record it or write it down.

Once back on campus, Liz sought out a piano in a vacant classroom and began picking out the melody. She practiced singing the song but was still stuck for the last line. She didn't want it to be the same as the last line of the first verse, as that was a question, and she wanted the song to end with an answer. And it had to be just right! She knew the general idea: *"If not I, who? If not now, when?"* She thought of another quote she had seen on a poster: *"I said, 'Somebody ought to do something!' Then I realized I* ***am*** *somebody!"* But that didn't fit into the song.

She again "gave it to the Lord" and returned to her apartment. Graduation was in a few days, and she needed to be getting packed up for the move back home. She wanted to get caught up on her sleep, since she had already been somewhat drained before she'd even taken the trip to Nashville. Exams in the theater department weren't like exams for other subjects, involving studying hundreds of pages of information. Theater exams usually involved demonstrating that the student not only knew about something but could actually *do* it. For Liz this had meant a three-hour session putting on makeup until her face resembled that of a large turtle, performing a monologue she had long ago memorized, and presenting to the costume design class her "plates" displaying her drawings of costumes for a Renaissance play. Liz remembered to thank the Lord for the ability to memorize easily and for the unusual level of inspiration and excitement about her ideas for the costume designs. She had pulled an "all-nighter" the week before out of sheer enthusiasm, and at the unveiling she could tell by the response that she had done well.

The only class she had outside the theater department that semester was an English course she was making up, having missed too much of it the first time, when she had had pneumonia. The "final" for that class was not an exam but a paper, and Liz had been given an extension because of the "death in the family." She looked forward to having it typed and turned in, so her last precious days in Urbana could be spent with her friends, especially Sean. She had so much to tell him!

Besides, her ring needed polishing again.

The next morning Liz sat in the late spring sunshine with her cup of coffee and her Bible opened to Isaiah.

"In the year that King Uzziah died," she read silently, *"I saw the Lord seated on a throne, high and exalted, and the train of his robe filled the temple."*[3] She paused for a moment and tried to visualize what Isaiah had seen and to absorb some of the awe of such a moment.

"High and exalted." What a contrast to her image of the Lord in a frail, twisted body. Could they really be one and the same? This kind of thought didn't bother her as much as it used to. After all, the words she was reading were written by the same prophet that described the Messiah as the Suffering Servant, *"despised and rejected by men, a man of sorrows and familiar with suffering."*[4] She had learned through what little Bible study she had done that Scripture was full of paradox. The same God who was high and exalted had come to earth lowly and meek. The God who had wiped out thousands of Israel's enemies had knelt to wash the feet of each of His disciples, including the one He knew would betray Him.

Liz was touched by such accounts of His humanity, especially after He had entered her life as "J," but she was also awed and fascinated by descriptions of Him as King of kings and Lord of lords.

"Above him were seraphs, each with six wings; with two wings they covered their faces, with two they covered their feet, and with two they were flying. And they were calling to one another:

"Holy, holy, holy is the LORD *Almighty;*
The whole earth is full of his glory.""[5]

She paused again, as a worship song she had just recently learned flooded her soul, and closing her eyes she smiled serenely, enjoying a verse of it before reading on.

"At the sound of their voices the doorposts and thresholds shook and the temple was filled with smoke." [6]

Wow… she thought, again trying to visualize such a thing.

Since her rebirth Bible reading had become daily habit. Some days Liz felt as thought she were doing it just because she should, because she wanted to please the Lord; she had learned that obedience doesn't require *feeling* like it.

This was not one of those days, however. Liz read with rapt attention the description of the Almighty in His glory and the intimidated response of His servant.

"'Woe to me!' I cried. 'I am ruined! For I am a man of unclean lips, and I live among a people of unclean lips, and my eyes have seen the King, the LORD Almighty.'

"Then one of the seraphs flew to me with a live coal in his hand, which he had taken with tongs from the altar. With it he touched my mouth and said, 'See, this has touched your lips; your guilt is taken away and your sin atoned for.'" [7]

What intensity! Liz thought. *And contrast*—the searing pain of lips touched with a live coal, then the infinite peace of being told, *"Your guilt is taken away and your sin atoned for."* Then, as though that weren't enough, *"Then I heard the voice of the Lord…"* To actually hear His voice—in that setting!—would be worth whatever pain preceded it, she thought.

"'Whom shall I send? And who will go for us?'" [8]

She read on, then stopped abruptly, her mouth dropping open. There it was!

Yes, that's it!

"Hey, guys, we've got something special for you tonight," Sean announced. "There's a reason we moved the meeting here tonight. We needed a piano. The Lord's given Liz a song, and she's gonna share it with us now." Sean had a way of getting to the point.

As the group murmured "awright!" and applauded, he winked at Liz and gave her the "thumbs up." Sheepishly she stepped over to the piano and sat down. Taking a deep breath, she began to play the haunting melody that had formed in her mind and heart on the airplane. Softly she began to sing.

"Staring out the window at the city far below,
I see endless rows of buildings full of people I don't know;
Though their malls and mills and mansions look like pebbles on the sand,
My Father knows each one of them; He holds them in His hand.

"But I wonder which ones know Him and which ones never will,
Which homes ring with laughter and which ones are cold and still.
And I wonder, who is hungry, and which ones have their fill?
If we don't share the Bread of Life with them, I wonder, then who will?"

The mood changed slightly as she began the second verse. The others in the room listened pensively; Liz's voice grew stronger as she gained confidence, and her hands stopped shaking.

"The Lord knows me, inside and out, every hair that's on my head;
And He knows the things I've done and felt, every word I've ever said.
And He knows the days ordained for me that He wrote down long before,
*And it amazes me that in that way, **He knows millions more!"***

She was quietly passionate as she sang,

"But I wonder who is crying, and which ones need a friend,
And where they'll spend eternity when their lives are at an end;
And I wonder, in this world of darkness, who will help them see?"

The music reached a crescendo and suddenly stopped. After a brief moment of silence, Liz closed the song with the line that had at first eluded her:

"Lord, here am I…
            …Send me." [9]

After the music faded out, there was a hush over the room, then applause. It wasn't thunderous applause, and Liz wondered whether her taking the spotlight had been a wrongly motivated waste of everyone's time. But as she shyly turned to the group, she noticed that they were smiling approvingly, and some had tears in their eyes. Sean was beaming proudly. Sarah's cheeks glistened, and as Liz got up from the piano, she met her halfway with a warm hug.

"Beautiful, Liz!" she whispered, then added with passion in her voice, "That *was* from God!"

"Do you realize how your prayers are being answered?" Sarah asked Liz later. "You were asking God if He wanted you to be like eyes in the Body of Christ, and He gives you that song!"

Liz was thinking about it and didn't answer, so Sean went on.

"I think the people here got it tonight. They really got it! I mean, they're seeing that their faith isn't just to soak up and enjoy, like most of us have been doing. There's a whole world of people out there that God wants us to reach out to."

"Yeah, that was the point of the song," Liz agreed.

"That song needs to be published!" Sarah was getting excited. "There's a guy in IV that sometimes writes songs and records them himself."

"I know who you mean," said Sean. "He's got this studio in his basement. I bet he'd record it for you."

"Wait, slow down," Liz protested. "I don't know anything about recording and selling songs."

"Neither do I, but I bet Jared knows all about it. He could help you."

"This close to finals and graduation?!" Liz cried. *This is crazy!* she thought.

"Hey, Jared lives in Alton. That's right in your neighborhood, isn't it?"

"Uh, yeah…"

"Maybe after graduation, you guys could get together and…"

What an adventure her life had become in the past couple of months! What a shame she hadn't begun a relationship with Jesus sooner, she thought, remembering nearly four years at the university as a timid, insecure theater student. Now it seemed her "comfort zone" was being stretched almost daily, and yet there was always some new thing just outside the zone to keep her guessing as to what He was going to come up with next. She was familiar with having butterflies in her stomach, but now the feeling wasn't so much fear as just excitement; while a part of her fretted, "I don't think I can do this!" the greater part, deeper and closer to God, was saying *"You're right, you can't—but He can!"* Then there would be the thrill of setting out for another unknown territory.

Like Colorado.

"So that's how I ended up here," Liz explained two months later. She was in a cabin in the Rocky Mountains with a bunkmate she had just met, a pretty, young aspiring singer named Jennifer. "Jared not only helped me with the demo recording, he told me about this seminar for Christian artists."

Jennifer popped the CD out of the CD player and handed it back to Liz. As she did, Liz noticed the long, perfect nails. The performer definitely had that polished look, which a few months earlier would have made Liz feel insecure and inferior. But now the two young women were chatting like old friends, finding out how much they had in common. Jennifer had sung an impressive number for Liz, and Liz had just shared her entry for the songwriting contest.

"My boyfriend Sean actually talked me into coming here," she told Jennifer. "He said it would be a good experience to learn more about songwriting, since I'm new at it."

"You mean that was your first song?" Jennifer asked, incredulous.

"Yeah," said Liz. "I sometimes don't even feel like it's *my* song, if you know what I mean…"

"Yeah, I know what you mean. Those are the best kind." Jennifer smiled. "I felt it was really anointed when you played it just now."

"There's that word again," said Liz. "What is *anointed*, anyway?" She added sheepishly, "I'm kind of a baby Christian, too."

"Really? Since when?" Jennifer's eyes sparkled with joy.

"I … I guess you could say I've always believed in the Lord, but I really came to know Him this spring. It's a long story. Maybe I can tell you about it sometime this week."

"I'd like that." Jennifer thought a moment. "Wow, so you've really had a big year! Saved, started writing songs—"

"And graduated from college. Funny how that seemed like such a major thing for so long, but once it happened it was pretty anticlimactic."

"Really?"

"Yeah. I went to a private, all-girls school until I graduated from high school, and there were only about sixty in my class. High school graduation was a big, big deal. We wore white dresses, carried bouquets—it was practically like getting married," she laughed. "But U of I had *thousands* graduating, and they didn't even read off all the names, much less hand us each a diploma. A lot of my friends didn't even go."

"Wow, how about that?" said Jennifer. "I still want to go back and finish my degree some day when I can afford it, but since I've known Jesus it doesn't seem as crucial as it did before. I just want to know what He wants for me."

"Yeah, me too. Don't you sometimes wish He'd just tell you instead of giving all these clues to figure out?"

Jennifer chuckled knowingly. "Yeah, you're like, 'Just give me a hint!'" The girls laughed. Liz thought, *How nice that we're each so unique, but we still can go through the same struggles and share a laugh over it.*

After a moment, Jennifer said, "It means having God's special touch on it."

"Huh?"

" 'Anointed.' It sort of means 'set aside specially,' or 'ordained by God.'"

"Oh … Cool." Liz grinned. "So you think God wants to use this song in a big way?"

"Maybe. It sure touched *me*."

"I'm hoping it'll touch a *lot* of people. I really want Him to use me!"

"Oh, He will, in one way or another. Hey, don't you have that meeting tonight?"

"Yeah, but it doesn't happen until 1:00. What kind of people have meetings at 1:00 in the morning?!" Liz complained jokingly.

"I guess people who are coming in from all over the country, maybe all over the world, and they wanted to make sure everyone had time to get here and unpack and get oriented."

"Yeah, I guess," Liz yawned. "But I've been traveling all day—car, plane, bus—and 1:00 A.M. is 2:00 A.M. St. Louis time!"

"But you must be anxious to see if your song's in the finals. It must be exciting."

"It is," Liz admitted. "I just wish I didn't have this headache. Oh well, I guess I could start heading over there."

"Good luck!" said Jennifer, who was starting to get undressed.

"Aren't you coming?" Liz asked.

"No, singers get judged during the seminar. So I get to be stressed out all week." She grinned. "I'll try to wait up for you, though. It's only midnight in California."

The meeting hall was packed with boisterous songwriters, most of them about Liz's age, some older, most of them with friends. *How can people have so much energy at this hour of the night?* she wondered. But then in spite of her headache, Liz felt a rush of nervous energy herself. The air was charged with it, with everyone's hope that tonight would begin a week of success that would launch them into a career in Christian music.

I don't know about "career," I just want You to use me, she prayed. Though she didn't know anyone and wished Sean could be there to share this moment with her, she did sense "J" at her side, holding her hand as the man with the paper came forward to announce the finalists in each category.

As he rattled off the titles of the finalists in each category, each title followed by whoops and cheers, Liz felt once again as if she were standing at the bulletin board at school, searching for her name among the cast of a new production. Only *this* time it was for Jesus. *This* time He'd use her, because this time "success" wasn't for her, it was for *Him,* and for the people who would be saved through the witness of listeners who were inspired by her song to "go forth into all the world…"

She listened intently, and as the man ran down the last list of titles, titles that didn't include "I Wonder Who Will," a growing sense of darkness seemed to engulf her. It was similar to the let-downs at Krannert Center, but much more intense and oppressive, almost palpable. Feeling as though she had been punched in the stomach by a prize fighter, she tried to catch her breath. She heard the man's voice, sounding oddly far away, announcing where the "losing" songs could be picked up. Each one had been judged by a panel of four judges and had been given a score, possibly some comments.

What followed was a chaotic scramble, as some people slapped one another on the back in congratulations, while others comforted, rationalized, philosophized, made excuses, or just flat-out cried. Liz had mixed feelings about being alone at this moment— glad her humiliation was not in front of people who knew her, yet badly needing a shoulder to cry on; Sean's would have been very welcome at the moment.

The many "losers" were anxious to see how their songs had scored, still hoping for some positive word of encouragement, and they grabbed their papers to devour any comments the professionals had written, like starving men seizing scraps of bread.

Liz found her song, a big "34" written at the top and no breakdown of the score, no comments written anywhere. *What's a "34"?* she wondered. Seeing the man who had made the announcements explaining something to a songwriter, she made her way over to him.

"Excuse me," she said. "What does the '34' at the top mean?" He looked at her as if she were not "all there."

"That's your score," he said. *Duh.*

"34 out of how many?" she asked. Thinly disguising his weariness, the man gave her a rather blank look. Obviously he was not one of the judges.

"Out of a hundred, I guess," he said with a shrug and walked away.

Oooof! Another blow to the stomach. Or was it the heart? Or head? Or all three? Liz had never received a grade lower than a 90% in her life, not even in theater. Yet inexplicably, rejection had been par for the course there. It had been painful there. Why was this so much worse?

As she headed back to the cabin, her mind was reeling, asking repeatedly, how could she have been so wrong? How could she not have had a clue—from God, her friends, anyone up until now—that this song was so poorly written and useless? Was she totally dense? The turmoil in her soul seemed so out of place in the peacefulness of the Rocky Mountain night. The freshness of the clean air smelled of God's creation; He was near. Yet how could she have been so out of touch with Him that she had to come all the way out here just to find out she had failed *again?!*

A hundred miles of walking later, she arrived at the cabin and unlocked the door. Stepping into the dimly lit room, she sighed, "Well, I didn't—"

She cut herself short, seeing that Jennifer had fallen asleep. She sighed again.

"Oh well, who cares anyway?" she muttered.

Although she was exhausted and had expected to sleep like a piece of petrified wood, sleep eluded her for hours. The little headache, which had now become a full-blown migraine, throbbed incessantly, and the rhythmic pounding seemed to scream into her brain,

... Loser! ... Loser! ... Loser! ... Loser! ...

And there, drowning in a flood of self-pity, she finally drifted off to sleep.

CHAPTER SIX

"For our struggle is not against flesh and blood, but against the rulers, against the authorities, against the powers of this dark world and against the spiritual forces of evil in the heavenly realms."—Ephesians 6:12

The meeting room was darkened by the forms of countless demons, summoned to an emergency council. As the last of the spirits to arrive fluttered in and lit upon the remaining rafters, their leader stood and motioned to them to be silent. There was an immediate hush, as every demon was anxious to learn what great threat to their kingdom would bring Lucifer himself from the battlefronts to such a relatively harmless place as the United States. Surely Apathy, Ignorance, Arrogance, and Ease had done a sufficient job of keeping the majority of the professing Christians in this affluent nation from being much of a force for the Kingdom of Heaven.

But today the Devil himself seemed disturbed enough to summon a myriad of demonic warriors, and they now awaited his instructions.

"As you all know", he began, "one of the most powerful forces both we and the Enemy have is music. You know how Lust, Addiction, and Suicide have made use of it in capturing and destroying a large part of this present generation."

Lust, Addiction, and Suicide looked at each other smugly, and for one brief moment there was a hint of satisfaction on Lucifer's face. But he then scowled as he continued:

"Unfortunately for us, there are also those in the Enemy's camp that are rediscovering its effectiveness and using it in ways that are snatching young humans away from us—some of the very ones we thought we had the tightest grip on!" His scaly talon clenched tightly, and as he began to pace, demons sheepishly backed out of his way.

"*This didn't seem that disastrous at first,*" he continued. "*We have succeeded in keeping the Enemy's music out of the mainstream music business, with the exception of some insipid, innocuous drivel. Only a small minority of the young population listen to the Real Thing. We've even managed to persuade some of the most talented of the Enemy's artists to "cross over" into neutral territory, from which it should be relatively simple to lure them over to our side completely, or at least render them totally ineffective.*"

"*So what's the problem?*" asked Complacency, wanting get to the point.

"*The problem,*" replied Lucifer, glaring at his subordinate, "*is that the few musicians who are really sold out to the Enemy are more and more realizing the power and opportunities they have at their fingertips, and how much more their side could have if they were to multiply themselves, and they're planning to do JUST THAT.*"

A murmur of dismay broke out among the demons, but they stopped momentarily in order to find out just what this ultimate battle plan might be.

"*A week-long seminar is being planned for this summer, one that will involve artists from all over the country and all over the world—singers, songwriters, instrumentalists, producers, technicians, publishers—you name it. Some of them are even people who used to be **our** tools and are now instruments in the hands of the Enemy. As if that weren't enough, now they plan on teaching and training others to be His instruments as well! Some of these creatures are people who don't even know the extent of their own talents yet! The Enemy is about to blow the lid off our whole Department of Blindness and Ignorance! Once these humans start realizing their potential and using it, it could be the beginning of the downfall of our whole kingdom!*" *His voice had risen in pitch, and some of the spirits looked at one another with questioning eyes. Seeing their puzzlement, Lucifer snapped at them.*

"*Think, fools!*" *he screamed.* "*There are still areas of this planet where preachers and missionaries aren't allowed to enter—but **musicians are**! And music draws people like a magnet, you know that from your own work. So, what we need now is a plan of counterattack.*"

"*Where are they meeting?*" asked Destruction, a large hulk of a demon that sat sharpening his nails and seemed relatively unconcerned. "*I'll just send a tornado and flatten the place the day before it's scheduled to start.*"

"*AMATEUR!*" shrieked Lucifer, whose anxiety had temporarily stripped him of his patience. "*Do you think you could stop them by knocking down a few buildings?*"

"*Destroy the people themselves,*" advised Death, a dark form that stood motionless in the shadows, "*or at least the ones who are the leaders. A well-timed bus crash right before the seminar could wipe out quite a piece of their army.*"

Lucifer sneered at him. "*Yes, and I suppose your crucifying the Enemy put an end to*

His battle plan? Don't be an idiot! We must avoid the obvious. Whatever we do, it must be subtle. Some of these people are real warriors of the Enemy, and if they were to recognize any of us, they could disarm us by using that detestable Name, and it would be the end of the mission for all of us! No, our plan must be carried out under cover—under the very Name of the Enemy Himself, if possible. You know that all our most successful plans have been carried out in the very Name of … in that Name." The multitude shuddered at the thought of the unspoken Name.

"I don't know about wiping out their whole plan," began Conformity, an intimidating demon with a scornful expression, "but we could really hem them into one place by narrowing their vision and destroying their sense of uniqueness. You know how successful my department has been in the past with our propaganda: 'Real Christians don't dance.' 'Real Christians don't wear makeup.' 'Real Christians dress like Americans.' Even 'Real Christians are white,'" he chuckled smugly.

"ENOUGH!" bellowed Lucifer. "You've been gloating over that Klan thing for decades. We're in a crisis here, and we need a plan we can implement **now**. How can your strategy limit these people?"

"Easy," replied Conformity. "Just get their eyes off the Enemy—that's always the first step.—and onto each other, especially onto the ones who are 'successful' by the world's standards." He motioned to three slimy creatures perched next to him who were picking their teeth with their skewer-like nails.

"Insecurity can help by getting them to deny who they really are while trying to imitate their idols. Blindness can get them to disregard the usefulness of their own unique qualities and instead try to compete with someone else who isn't like them at all. Then after the inevitable happens, Frustration can come in and plunder the remains."

"Sounds like a piece of cake to me," Frustration commented with a grin, and Insecurity added, "No problem! Musicians are so insecure anyway; I could pull this off on my lunch hour."

"Why stop there?" hissed Cruelty from the shadows. "All these ideas are rather vague, and as musicians are a pretty moody bunch, why don't we provide a more concrete way of destroying their self-worth, rather than relying on bad feelings that could be brushed away with a prayer?" He paused, and his eyes gleamed with the evil inspiration that was beginning to take shape. "Get them to judge one another in a very limited setting, and have them put that judgment **in writing**. It will drive some of them to the brink of suicide!" His mouth watered at the very thought of so much misery.

Confusion jumped in. "I'll instruct my imps to put it into the mind of every artist to question his or her gift on the basis of those pieces of paper!"

"B-but surely," reasoned a small spirit in the back of the room, "they'll know that any art form is a matter of taste and human opinion, and that those tastes vary from person to person, even from day to day in the same person. I mean, hasn't each of them seen the Enemy work through their individual gifts already? They must know their talents are from Him … Don't they?"

"You'd be amazed," replied an older demon named Moody, "how quickly an artist can forget these things when confronted with an immediate Failure."

"Yes, especially when 'Failure' is defined by someone who is 'Recognized in the Business,' yet knows little or nothing about the individual he's judging, or that person's calling," added Intimidation with cool confidence.

"Meanwhile," Fear interjected, "all the anxiety we can produce in such a situation can cause a lack of sleep and health—"

"Sounds convenient to me," muttered Sickness.

"—which may not be all that crucial to our cause, but it wouldn't hurt it, either."

"And," added Cruelty, quivering with pleasure, "it is such fun to watch the creatures suffer." There was a wave of chuckles through the crowd, but suddenly an old demon that until now had been silent spoke up.

"Careful," he cautioned them. "I've known these plans to backfire in my time. When humans are hurt and humiliated, it often happens that they draw closer to the Enemy in their humility—You know how He likes… humility!" he spat the word in disgust. "… and also that they can empathize and comfort one another. There's a danger of not only maturity but closeness and love resulting …"

There was a low murmuring of distaste at the "L" word throughout the room, until Pride spoke out loudly and confidently.

"Never fear!" he assured them. "I'll see to it that none of them admit their hurt to one another. I have plenty of imps that will scatter and persuade every last one of them to put on a mask of super-spirituality …"

"While all the time envying the 'successful'!" hissed Worldliness.

"And feeling inadequate!" squealed Inferiority.

"And finally giving up trying to do anything at all with their gifts!" Despair shrieked triumphantly. The four began dancing with glee.

"HOLD ON!" bellowed Lucifer. He wanted to think this through; it seemed too easy. "What about the few who come out on top? It didn't take many disciples to turn the world upside down before. What if the winners …"

"We'll take care of them, Sir!" chimed in a rowdy chorus of demons that included Arrogance, Lust, Greed, Conceit, and Self-centeredness.

The Devil gazed at the room full of spirits, poised in readiness for his orders, some trembling with eagerness, their claws at their swords, and a cruel smile spread across his face.

"Then do what you have to do," he ordered, his fiery eyes narrowing. "Poison this plan in its very inception, and we'll maintain control over the music world. After all, it was given to **me**, and I have no intention of letting it go."

And so it came to pass that as a group of godly leaders gathered to plan a week that would change the world, an unseen, uninvited band of spirits joined them. It included Conformity with his passion for cloning, Competitiveness with his loathing of unity, and Greed, Worldliness, and Ambition, all disguised in the most spiritual clothes. Meanwhile, Intimidation, Discouragement, Confusion, Depression, Despair, and many others all sharpened their swords, preparing to finish off the multitudes of wounded who were bound to be everywhere by the end of the summer.

Several of the demons surrounded one member of the group whose mind had been distracted during the prayer. As they dug invisible talons into his brain, he gasped, not with pain, but with a sudden inspiration he thought was from God.

"I've got a great idea!" he cried, while the spirits smiled at one another with evil satisfaction. "Let's hold competitions!"

"When you ask, you do not receive, because you ask with wrong motives, that you may spend what you get on your pleasures."—James 4:3

Liz sat up in bed with a gasp. It was just after dawn, and the early sunlight filtered through the dingy curtains of the cabin. Her head still ached relentlessly, and as she buried her face in her hands, all the depressing realities of the night before came rushing back to her consciousness without mercy.

A groan came from the bottom bunk, and the bed shook and creaked as Jennifer rolled over and stretched.

"G'morning," she said in a voice that was sleepy yet cheery, and Liz noticed that they could see each other in the dresser mirror. Liz straightened up but not soon enough to hide her pain. "You Okay?" Jennifer asked with concern.

"I've got a splitting headache."

"Another one?"

"Same one."

"Poor girl! Didn't you take anything for it?"

"No, I didn't have anything."

"Well, why didn't you say so?" Jennifer scolded, jumping up and heading for the bathroom. She disappeared around the corner, and Liz could hear her rummaging through her bag. "What do you take? Tylenol? Advil?"

"Either one's fine," said Liz, rubbing her forehead. She heard the water running, and soon Jennifer came out with the pills and a mug that had flowers and a Bible verse on it.

"Thanks. That's sweet of you."

"No problem. Hey, how'd it go last night?"

"Lousy. I didn't even make the first cut."

"Oh, I'm sorry," said Jennifer with genuine empathy.

"Yeah, me too. Then I saw the grade they gave me: 34."

"Is that bad?"

"34 out of a hundred? I'd say so."

"*Ouch!* Where'd they get that? That's terrible!"

"You're telling me. I thought I'd at least learn something, but there weren't any comments on it, so I have no idea why I did so badly."

"Well, what do they know anyway?" said Jennifer with exaggerated scorn.

"Apparently plenty. Tell me the truth, Jennifer. What did you *really* think of it?"

"I told you the truth. I *loved* it. I'd sing it any day."

"Would you really?"

"Really. Just remember, Satan's a cockroach with a megaphone."

"Huh?" Something about the comment sounded vaguely familiar to Liz, like a recent dream.

"Think about it. C'mon, let's get some breakfast." Liz wasn't the least bit hungry; the migraine had made her positively nauseous, but something about Jennifer's company was healing and refreshing, and Liz wasn't ready to be alone again just yet.

The dining hall was surprisingly quiet for the number of people that filled it that morning. Many looked tired from traveling, staying up late, and receiving news that was either too exciting to let one sleep, or so depressing that a good night's sleep wouldn't have helped. Liz and Jennifer introduced themselves to the others at their table, who in turn introduced themselves. Then everyone found out where everyone was from— L.A., Dallas, New York, Chicago—and whether they were singers, songwriters, or just there for the nightly entertainment. "Big name" singers from the Christian music industry were coming to perform every night. There was also to be a service every morning after breakfast, one at noon, and opportunities to attend Bible studies and hear well-known speakers. Liz decided just to forget the songwriting fiasco and try to enjoy the week as a time of spiritual growth and renewal, as well as the beauty of the Rocky Mountains in the summer and the fellowship of so many other Christians from all over.

A familiar-looking man stepped up to the microphone and requested everyone's attention; he had some announcements to make. There were a few changes in times and locations of some of the workshops. He ran down the list, then added, "Y'know, this morning I noticed some tears in here, and I knew right away they had to be songwriters." There was a soft murmur of knowing laughter throughout the dining hall, and the man went on. "I just hope that while you're praying today, you'll remember to pray for the losers. They're feelin' pretty bad."

"We'd feel better if you'd stop calling us 'losers'!" the man from New York muttered under his breath, and the diners within earshot nodded and chuckled, "Amen!"

Liz thought about how bad she had felt the night before and how alone she had felt in her misery. Then looking around the room, she realized that probably half the people there felt as bad as she did! And by the end of the week, all but about ten of them would be in the same boat, wearing the same title: "Loser." *How sad!* she thought. *Especially since these are God's children, and they're just trying to serve Him!*—or were they? She was disturbed to find that she felt bad for another reason besides the evident pain of so many people. She looked at the numbers and realized she was not only a loser, she was "*just another* loser." She was nothing special.

Was that the reason for her pursuing success—to prove she was special? She knew she was; she also knew every person there was, too. Had she wanted to be a little more special than the others? The image of a demon named Pride flashed across her mind, and another piece of her dream returned to her.

Hmmm ... Maybe there was a reason for her to be here that had nothing to do with her song per se. *OK, Lord, just show me ...*

After the first session of the songwriting workshop, Liz lingered, hoping to gain some feedback from one of the people whose wisdom she had come so far to hear. Two or three other people gathered around the lecturer; apparently they had had the same idea.

A lady was watching anxiously as the instructor took a piece of paper from her. She glanced at the top a moment. "I don't know what this song is about," she commented with a hint of impatience.

"W-well, that comes out later ... It's kind of a ..."

The instructor handed the paper back to the bewildered woman. "I have to know what the song's about."

" .. surprise ..." the lady finished the sentence unheard as the professional took a paper from another songwriter. Obviously intimidated, she turned to go. Expecting that she herself would have the same reaction to the instructor, only with less boldness, Liz found herself leaving with the young woman.

"She didn't even read it," Liz observed. The flustered songwriter seemed to feel she had to explain.

"I thought it would be sorta neat not to let people know right away what it's about. You know, keep 'em wondering, or spark their curiosity, or whatever." She sighed. "I guess that wasn't such a great idea."

"Oh, I don't know," Liz said cheerfully. "I like surprises." She thought of a country song that had always made her laugh, where the man was singing lovingly about how special "she" was, and how proud he was to be seen with "her," only to let on at the end that he was not singing about his woman but about his car. She reached for the girl's song. "May I?" she asked.

"If you want," the woman replied half-heartedly, handing her the neatly printed song. Liz read:

"You were there when I entered this dark, stormy life;
Your love was there to light my way.
You taught me ABCs and that Jesus loves me,
How to live, how to love, and how to pray. (*About her mom?* Liz wondered.)

"You were there to pronounce us husband and wife; (*About her minister?*)
You were the one who gave me away. (*Her dad must be a minister!*)
You helped weather the storm when the babies were born;"
(*Must be quite a dad!*)
"Together we watch our children play. [Refrain]"

"No matter where I go, it seems I see you there,
A reminder of God's love and grace;
And I always get this feeling I know you very well,
Though you have a different voice, a different face." (*Hmmm ... !*)

"I'm always glad to see you the day that we first meet,
And I'm always crying when it's time to go;
But the Lord holds us together when we pray for one another;
I even hear you on the radio!"

"Wow. I give up!" Liz laughed.
"Keep going," the girl said. "The refrain explains it."

"Refrain:
You sing me songs, you make me laugh, you cry with me;
You're my brother, you're my sister, tried and true.
In all the places I have gone, you were there, so I was home.
You're the Body of Christ, and I love you."

"Oh, it's about the Church!" Liz exclaimed with delight.

"So … what do you think?" the woman asked apprehensively.

"Well, I may not know anything about songwriting, but I know what I like, and I like this."

"Really?" the songwriter sounded doubtful.

"Really. It's too bad she didn't read the whole thing," Liz added. She handed the song back, and they continued walking. "I'm not sure I get her. She wanted to know immediately what your song was about, but the example she kept using of a good songwriter was Paul Simon, and some of his songs *really* confuse me!"

"You mean you don't understand what 'Call Me Al' is about?!" The lady laughed; it was the first time Liz had seen her smile. They reached a fork in the road, and she said, "I gotta go pick up my kids from the camp."

"Oh … OK, 'bye!" said Liz. "Maybe I'll see you later."

" 'Bye—and thanks."

For what? Liz wondered. Then she realized she may have cheered up a very depressed child of God. Maybe it was just a Band-Aid, but it was something.

OK, so maybe I won't be a world-famous gospel songwriter, she thought, *but that doesn't mean God can't use me.* The thought became a prayer. *OK, Lord, use me all You want.*

A lot of healing is needed here.

Was that her prayer, or was that God's voice?

After the noon chapel service the restroom line wound all the way out the door, so there was a bit of a wait. Liz tried to make small talk with the woman ahead of her. "Are you enjoying the seminar?" she asked.

The woman's expression clearly said "No," and she sighed dejectedly. "Well, I'm *learning* a lot!" she replied with a note of bitterness in her voice. Liz saw in her tired face the same pain she had been feeling and wondered just what this woman had "learned"—that she was a failure? That God couldn't or wouldn't use her? As flashes of her dream came back to her, it seemed that in large part the enemy's plan was working, and it made her angry.

"Try to remember Who it is that you're representing," a big-name singer admonished the crowd that night when he'd finished singing. "I was talking with one of the workers here, and she said, 'Do you know what we call this week? Hell Week.' Of course, I wanted to know why, and she told me. 'Because Christians are the rudest, most self-centered, demanding people who come here!'" —*Ouch!*— "'And they're by far the worst tippers!'"

It dawned on Liz that at meals, with all the worrying and fretting and commiserating with the other wounded egos, she (and how many others?) hadn't even thought about those who were providing the food, the service, the clean-up.

"It really hurts," the singer went on, "to know people feel that way about us, and how much it hurts the Lord. So while you're here to receive, don't forget to give, too. People are watching us to see what He's like. Let's change that opinion to a good one. God bless you. Good night." Although the star had appeared on stage accompanied by music, lights, and fog, he left rather abruptly, with no fanfare. The audience was more subdued than they had been all evening, having been rebuked, and, one would hope, convicted.

Liz felt a sudden urge to get out of the crowd. Overwhelmed with a sudden weariness, she made her way through the people and out the door just as another group was coming on stage to perform. The floorboards vibrated with the volume of their opening notes as the sound almost pushed Liz out the door. As she walked away from the concert, she noticed for the first time that her ears were ringing. The sensation brought back a wave of memories from her high school days of coming home from a rock concert with burning eyes and the smell of smoke (tobacco and otherwise) on her clothes. She was glad her cabin was far enough away from the concert hall that the walk in the mountain air could refresh her body and soul before she would tumble into bed in a relatively quiet place.

Soon the mountains themselves began to muffle the man-made sounds. In the concert hall the performers on stage had seemed larger than life, the light shows and high-tech sound impressive and expansive. Now as Liz turned to look back down the valley, she saw that the building itself was already looking small against the prodigious mountains that stood like silent giants, silhouetted against a purple sky. She realized with shame that she had been so intent on her present interests that she hadn't taken the time to admire God's handiwork which was all around. She had been rather sulky about the fact that people didn't seem to appreciate *her song,* yet here was unappreciated creation all around, crafted by the mighty Creator with such love and genius and originality—everything from the tiny wildflowers that adorned the mountainside to the creek that tumbled over the multicolored stones, to the majestic peaks of the Rockies. And other than a momentary gasp of wonder when she had first exited the bus from the airport, she had pretty much passed through it all without a second thought. She stopped to apologize to Him and to take it all in.

She was far enough away from the lights and the music that she could hear the night breeze whispering through the pine trees that towered over her, and see a million stars twinkling against a black velvet sky.

"Lord, You're awesome!" she whispered. The breeze caressed her cheeks, and she couldn't help smiling. Farther up the hill she could hear more music, but it bore very little similarity to the star-studded performances being enjoyed by the multitude in the valley. A lone guitar played, and about half a dozen voices around a campfire sang "Amazing Grace." Liz continued to gaze at the night sky, quietly singing along as a feeling of gratitude and peace swept over her.

Somehow Liz felt the presence of God more in that moment that she had all day.

Back at the cabin, Liz continued to be aware of the presence of Jesus, not the Jesus glorified that night with laser lights and other special effects, but more the "J" she had grown to love in a dream, the Friend whose body was blind and crippled with cerebral palsy. It was then that the words came back to her.

"The stingiest tippers!" She pictured His fingers curled up, the hands refusing to open, no matter how badly He wanted them to.

She pictured the little boy with cerebral palsy she had seen Sarah working with when she had set out in search of her Friend from the dream. How he had cried in frustration because his body wouldn't do what he wanted it to!

How frustrated You must be with us! she cried in her spirit.

Lord, she prayed that night, *help me to help open Your hands—help me to* **remember***! When I get so self-centered, I forget all about others. Oh Lord,* she moaned, *deliver me from* ***self****!*

CHAPTER EIGHT

The following morning Liz decided to attend the second session of a workshop led by two singers, one whom she had heard often and one whose name was vaguely familiar to her. She had been told that in their first session these two were refreshingly honest about all the hoopla regarding the industry, and they had encouraged each person to seek where *God* wanted to use them—and *yes, He would,* whether in the spotlight or hidden, whether in America or in a remote part of the world where the Word of God was so desperately needed. They had mentioned names unknown to Liz and to most Americans for that matter, but well-known in other countries, and most importantly well-known in heaven. For perspective, they related how these "failures" in the eyes of the Western music business had led thousands to Christ through their ministry. This sounded like a good workshop to go to for getting priorities in order, Liz decided.

Apparently many others had had the same idea. People squeezed into the couches and sat cross-legged on the floor, so Liz had to step over some to get to where Jennifer was saving her a spot.

"Excuse me," she apologized to the people who had to scrunch up to make room for her to step through.

Give that girl a hug.

The impression was not audible, but it was very clear. Liz glanced over to see a young girl, maybe twenty years old, seated on a couch with someone who appeared to be her mother. She didn't seem to be particularly needy, just someone waiting for the workshop to start. Liz started to continue making her way toward her spot.

HUG HER!

I'd have to step back over those people! Liz argued with herself—or was she arguing with God? That would be a futile thing to try to do. *Oh, OK …*

"Excuse me," she said again to the same people as she backtracked to the couch where the girl sat. Their eyes met, and Liz had the feeling her face was flushed. The girl looked mildly curious.

"Uh, could I … give you a hug?" Liz stammered.

"Uh … sure …" the girl responded.

Liz hugged her, and to her surprise, the girl hugged her back. When Liz again looked into her eyes, she was even more surprised to see they were brimming over with tears.

"Oh, I needed that!" she said to Liz in a choked voice.

"I know," Liz smiled sympathetically. **Now I know,** she thought.

How many, Lord?!

Too many. By the time the leaders were ready to start there were people standing outside, looking through the windows because the cabin was literally packed wall-to-wall. They blushed when the female leader mentioned the pain of losing in competition, and they chuckled sheepishly as she affectionately scolded, "You set yourselves up for it!" The crowd listened in rapt silence as the pair of singers told of the abundance of ministries involving music. Writing and singing songs for American recording companies was certainly not the only way to use musical gifts! Liz pondered her own narrow-minded view of "success" as she heard listed the many "mission fields" that most Christians had no interest in, for reasons that were embarrassingly obvious: giving a free concert in the inner city, traveling to a remote country to minister to people dying of AIDS, singing to and with handicapped children, serenading a nursing home; the list went on. None of these was very glamorous or lucrative, and the people were left to contemplate their motivation. Was their passion really for Jesus, or was it for self-glory, riches and fame? So, at the end of the hour, while Liz and the others dispersed, presumably to their "prayer closets," they were comforted by the thought that perhaps they hadn't failed in their music after all. Yet perhaps they also had the uncomfortable conviction that they had failed in a much more serious area, and that for all their "spiritual" talk, they had actually put their own hopes and dreams ahead of His will.

Liz decided to spend some time just seeking God and setting aside the "business" for a while. She was glad Sean had advised her to bring her guitar in spite of her being convinced she'd never have time to use it. She returned to the cabin to get it along with her Bible. She stuffed some Kleenex in her pocket, aware that she was prone to tears at the most unexpected times, and was about to walk out the door when she thought she'd probably want to hit the gift shop before lunch. Taking one of the last two twenty-dollar bills out of her wallet, she stuffed it in her pocket and set out to find a good place to meet with her Best Friend.

She found a "prayer closet" that resembled a closet about as much as a canyon resembles a recording studio. Seated on a mossy rock by a mountain stream, she watched the sunlight sparkling off the crystal-clear water that tumbled down over the various colored stones. It amazed her that as she sat in the summer heat, there was still snow melting somewhere up that mountain, yet she could see on distant peaks that there were still patches of white; how high she didn't know. The sheer hugeness of them reminded her again how big God was, and how small she was in comparison. She was still in awe that He could care about her so much that He would speak to her personally in so many ways.

'What is man that You are mindful of him?'[1] she wondered with the Psalmist.

It was a time where the Psalms seemed appropriate, their verses of wonder at God's creation, their multiplicity of emotions, their familiar verses that reminded Liz of songs she had sung in church. After reading enough Psalms to be overwhelmed with the majesty of God, she got out her guitar, grinning as she resisted the urge to belt out a line about the hills' being alive with the sound of music. Performing in that musical at the university seemed like yesterday, yet a million years ago.

As Liz sang with a voice that the "professionals" at the conference would no doubt find insufficient, she still had the feeling the One who had given her that voice was glad to hear it singing His praises. Breezes whispered through the pine trees in response and caressed her cheek lovingly. She closed her eyes and drank in the warmth of the moment. It seemed that "J" was repeatedly sending little tokens of love to delight her, such as the chipmunk that came up and eyed her curiously, its nose twitching. When Liz couldn't contain a laugh at the overstuffed cheeks, it scampered away. Feeling the cooling shadow of a cloud, she looked up just in time to see an eagle soaring overhead. Sky-blue columbine swayed in the breeze. Liz heard the snap of a twig close by. Cautiously she turned her head and stifled a gasp. There, not twenty feet away was something she had never seen up close, a young doe. Its liquid brown eyes met hers, and with a flick of its tail it bounded back into the woods.

"Thanks, Lord," Liz said out loud. "I've enjoyed the show." As if in answer, the sky rumbled, and Liz noticed how dark the approaching clouds were. She headed back for the cabin to return her Bible and guitar. Checking her watch, she realized it was later than she had thought. In fact, she had so lost track of time that she would not have time to stop by the gift shop before lunch, so she headed straight for the dining hall. As she reached the end of the path, she felt a drop of rain and was grateful she had made it without getting soaked.

Inside, she picked up a tray and got in line behind a group of strangers. She searched the room for Jennifer but found no familiar faces except those of the kitchen staff who were dishing up the food and bussing tables. One woman who appeared to be in her mid-thirties, seemed particularly weary, and Liz recalled the singers' convicting words the night before. She didn't notice anyone else giving the woman any encouragement; on the contrary, they acted as if she didn't exist—pretty much the way Liz had acted the day before. Whispering a prayer, Liz got her food, thanked the server, and approached the place the woman had just wiped clean.

"Thanks," she said. "I don't know how you keep up with us."

The woman looked at her as if not sure Liz was talking to her. Liz looked into her face and smiled.

"So many people here, and the place still sparkles! You all do a great job. We appreciate it."

The woman blinked, hesitated a moment, then with a smile said quietly, "Well, thank you." As she went to clean the spot next to Liz, there was a subtle change in her, noticeable perhaps only to Liz. It was something in her eyes, or maybe it was a bit more energy in her step as she walked away. Whatever it was, Liz realized that all people need encouragement and appreciation, whatever their job. She made up her mind to give at least one sincere compliment each time she went through the line. However demanding, self-centered and arrogant some other Christians were—and she herself had been—she was determined not to contribute any more to the perception of "Hell Week" the rest of the time she was there.

"Hi Liz," came a voice that was familiar yet somewhat lacking in energy. Liz had been so lost in thought watching the kitchen staff and taking in what she felt God saying to her that she hadn't seen Jennifer come in.

"Jennifer! Have a seat!" she greeted her, pulling out the chair next to her. She was surprised to hear the cheerfulness in her own voice, and it was clear to her that her time with God had made a difference in her outlook. Jennifer, however, set down her tray without another word and bowed her head, presumably to ask a blessing. A moment later Liz heard a sigh and as Jennifer lifted her head, saw unmistakable tears.

"Well, I'm out," she said in a voice that betrayed hurt in spite of her attempts at sounding cavalier.

"You got eliminated?" Liz blurted, then mentally kicked herself. *Duh!*

"I guess I'm not professional material. Oh well. If it's not God's will, it's not His will," Jennifer shrugged and picked at her food with her fork.

Liz knew how hard it was to see the bright side at such a time. Even if one acknowledged intellectually that God knew what was best, still emotionally…

"But it still hurts like heck," she empathized. Jennifer said nothing. "It's OK to admit it, Jen."

"Yeah, I guess I'm not fooling Him, am I?" She laughed through her tears, put down her fork, and dabbed at her eyes with her napkin. "I'm not really hungry. I think I need to go back to the cabin. I've got some praying to do."

"I understand."

Jennifer stood to go.

"… Jennifer?"

"Yeah?"

"I love your voice. I hear God when you sing."

Jennifer bit her lip and shut her eyes to hold back the tears. "Thanks, Liz."

"And can I have your cookie?"

Jennifer laughed in spite of herself, rolled her eyes, shook her head, and tossed the cookie to Liz.

"Here, knock yourself out."

"Thanks," Liz smirked.

As she started for the door, Jennifer noticed the kitchen staff hustling to keep up with the changing shifts of diners. "Hey Liz, I forgot to bring something for a tip. You got anything?"

"Uh, not really," Liz began. Then, slipping her hand into her pocket, she said, "Oh, wait, yes I do. Don't worry about it." Jennifer smiled, waved goodbye, and left.

It occurred to Liz that before she and Jennifer had been "eliminated," neither of them had given much thought to the workers. *"Stingiest tippers."* The words stung just as much in her memory as hearing them for the first time. *Not today,* she thought. *I don't need any souvenirs anyway.* She remembered from French class that "souvenir" means "memory." Her important memories of the seminar were already written in her journal, and the most important of all were etched on her heart.

After a pleasant lunch with another songwriter and the family of a singer who was leading a workshop, Liz lingered at the table, nibbling the chocolate chip plunder and saying a prayer for Jennifer, for all the others inappropriately labeled "losers," and for any workers who might still be seeing Christians as the most self-centered people they ever had the misfortune to work with.

She thought of "J," how He had appeared in her dream with handicaps that rendered Him unattractive to the casual observer. His body had given a false impression of what He was really like, the wise and loving Friend. And if the church, being the Body of Christ, gave the world a false impression of who He was, how would the world ever really know Him? The retreat center was full of people presumably aspiring to glorify God with their songs, instruments, and voices, preferably glorifying Him before millions of people at a time.

But forget the crowds of fans. What about the waiter? The cab driver? The clerk in the store? The cleaning lady? If self-obsessed Christians routinely treated individuals like dirt, how would those individuals ever know there was God who valued them enough to die for them?

God help us! she cried silently.

A loud clap of thunder woke her from her meditations, and she realized she was the only guest left in the dining hall. The food was being put away, and the lady she had spoken to earlier was mopping the floor.

"You'd better get going, Hon, you're gonna be late," she admonished. Something about the way she called Liz "Hon" gave her a warm feeling and reminded her of what she had intended to do earlier. When the lady's back was turned, Liz took out the twenty-dollar bill and slipped it onto the table between the salt and pepper shakers.

Suddenly the sound of pouring rain hitting the roof made her come to the embarrassing realization that she was unprepared for the change in the weather.

"Yipes! I didn't bring a raincoat or umbrella!" She smacked herself on the forehead.

"'Yipes' is right. It's really coming down out there. How far is your cabin?"

"About as far away as it can be and still be in Colorado."

"You'd better wait 'til the rain lets up some."

Another worker, a motherly-looking woman in her fifties who had been wiping off tables, came over to where the two were talking. "Is there a problem, Julie?" she asked.

"This lady doesn't have any raingear," her coworker explained.

"I'm just waiting for it to let up," Liz added, blushing.

"You're gonna be waiting a long time, by the looks of it," the older one commented. "—Hey, I have an idea!" she exclaimed, her face brightening.

"Where you goin', Maggie?" Julie asked.

"You'll see!" Maggie's voice faded out as she disappeared into the kitchen. A moment later she emerged with a large black plastic bag and a pair of scissors.

"We'll just make you a poncho!" she announced. Liz watched awkwardly as the ladies cut a hole in the bag for her head then started to put it on her.

"Not yet! What about her arms?" Maggie scolded Julie. All three began to laugh as the garment took shape.

"Not exactly Glamour magazine material," commented Julie.

"Are you kidding? It's a masterpiece!" Maggie retorted.

"Hey, I always wanted to be a trend-setter," Liz laughed, turning from side to side like a model on a runway.

Maggie produced another bag from her pocket and handed it to Liz.

"Here, Honey, put this over your head. It's not an umbrella, but it'll keep you from getting *too* soaked."

Liz took the bag and impulsively hugged the two ladies. "Thanks so much! You're the best!" she cried.

The last thing she saw as she ran out into the rain was that the smiles on the ladies' faces were bright and real, not those of annoyed workers putting up with an incompetent guest.

CHAPTER NINE

"I have so much to tell you," Liz told Sean over the phone. She sighed. "I wish you were here." The sound of his voice had intensified her homesickness. "I'm learning so much, not just about the music business, but about me."

"Really?" Sean replied. He did not sound surprised.

"Yeah, and I'm not at all sure I like what I'm learning."

"Hey, you'll be OK," Sean assured her. "You're just getting an attitude adjustment. It happens all the time."

"*All* the time?" Liz groaned.

"Yep. Sorry. Get used to it," he advised with mock coldness.

"I can't wait to see you," she said, changing the subject.

"Just one more day! Hang in there. Hey, my parents can't wait to meet you!"

"I hope you haven't given me too much of a buildup. I'd hate to disappoint them."

"What are you talking about?" he scolded.

"I'm gonna be exhausted, I'm afraid—not exactly looking my best."

"Hey, my family's not exactly beauty contest winners, either. Big deal. They're gonna love you…like I do."

"I love you, too!—oops, my battery's running low, I guess I'd better go."

"OK, kiddo, see ya soon!"

Liz was glad she had planned her return trip to include a stopover in Chicago. She was anxious to see Sean, for reasons that varied with her emotions. She had so much to tell him! She had been learning first-hand about God's priorities, and He had reinforced these lessons by working through her in unexpected ways. She was excited and happy about the serendipity she had experienced in the one-on-one encounters throughout the week.

On the other hand, the pain of the dream that had been shattered the first night would come back at equally unexpected moments, that little demon called Rejection whose specialty it was to kill a person's joy with unrealistic expectations. For no matter how much Liz told herself that her song would not be published and change the world, and that that was OK, somewhere deep down she hoped the Lord would recognize the sacrifice she was making and reward her humble attitude by giving her the very thing she had been willing to give up. And of course the fact that she couldn't seem to shake that hope for good (and the irony of occasional moments of being proud of her humility) proved that Ambition had once more crawled off the altar.

She was disgusted with herself for being so selfish and shallow after all she had seen and learned, but she seemed powerless to change herself permanently. So she was left with the only thing she could realistically hope for, and in fact probably the best thing to hope for—that God Himself would eventually deliver her from all worldly tendencies.

So, while she looked forward to sharing all her enlightening experiences with Sean, she also just longed to feel his arms around her and feel accepted, knowing that he loved and respected and esteemed her more than anyone at the seminar had. Somehow conversations on the cell phone didn't quite satisfy.

As Liz turned off her cell phone, Jennifer appeared in the doorway.

"Hi, Liz—Oh, I'm sorry—" She covered her mouth when she saw the phone.

"It's OK, I was just finished. Sean and I just wore out the battery again." Jennifer chuckled.

"Hey, you know how you were so frustrated because you didn't get any feedback on your song?"

"Yeah…"

"Some of the songwriters have been going to this workshop with some people in the music industry, and they've been getting their input."

"Really?"

"Yeah, they get together one more time tomorrow. You might want to take in your song and see what they say."

"Hmm…" Liz had mixed feelings. It was bad enough getting rejected on paper. Did she really need to be humiliated again, face to face, in front of a group of her peers?

"Hey, how often do you get a chance to get evaluated by professionals?" Jennifer reasoned. Liz cringed at the "p" word she was starting to hate.

"I guess I should go and get some guidance for future songs."

"There you go! When you get back, I'll have a quart of Ben and Jerry's to drown our sorrows in."

"Sounds good, I guess. ..'our?' You mean you're still…"

"…dealing with it? Yeah, I am."

Liz glanced anxiously at her watch as the panel of experts evaluated a song by a young man from Texas. Her song was the last on the list and would be critiqued "if there's time." At first she was almost hoping there wouldn't be, but as the hour passed and she heard other songwriters being advised, she realized that she was probably no less gifted than any of them, and that criticism wasn't fatal. At least no one had died yet. Some of them had even slipped out after their own critiques, so the potential "audience" had shrunk considerably.

"OK, last we have," the man read the label, " 'I Wonder Who Will.'" Liz's pulse quickened as he put the CD in the player, and she could feel her face redden when she heard her own voice on the recording, something she had never quite got used to hearing. She glanced around the room as subtly as she could to see if she could discern any response. Maybe the Lord would use her words to inspire someone in the room to reach out. If He did, and if that person went on to lead someone—anyone—to Christ, then it would all be worth it.

But of the songwriters who had remained, four of them were absorbed in reading their written evaluations, one was looking at her watch, and two were engaged in silent conversation, scribbling notes to each other. Liz was disappointed that no one seemed to be paying attention, but she had to admit that she herself had only halfheartedly listened to the others.

There it is, **self** *again,* she thought. *It seems to be a universal condition.*

"So what did they say?" Jennifer wanted to know back at the cabin.

"Not a lot. I got the feeling they were tired. It was the very last song on the last day. They suggested I change a word here and there, but as for anything substantial, all I got was one of them saying, 'Frankly, I just can't relate to this song.' It's about the Great Commission, for heaven's sake! And he can't relate?"

"Maybe if he related, he'd be on the mission field instead of in the board room," Jennifer mused. Liz thought about it for a moment.

"So, how do we do it? I mean, we want to reach as many people as possible, but when—*if*—we get mass exposure, suddenly we're in the middle of this world system—professionals, business, strategy, P.R.—ego, greed, and *selfishness!* It gives me a whole new appreciation for the artists that can be famous and still keep their focus. How do they do it? How do they reach so many people without getting caught up in that other stuff?"

"They pray," said Jennifer. "They pray a *lot.*"

"Then we should, too, I guess."

The girls joined hands and prayed long and sincerely, for themselves, for each other, for the artists that were "going places," for the ones just going home, heartbroken. They prayed for the "successful" and for the lost souls who would be reached by them and their recordings. And as they prayed, their own heartaches slowly began to melt away, as did the Ben and Jerry's, forming a sweet, creamy puddle on the sink and dribbling down the drain.

The seminar ended differently from the way Liz would have imagined a week before. There were hugs from Maggie and Julie after breakfast the day she left; Maggie even said how much she had "enjoyed having you all here this week," and Liz said a silent prayer of thanks. She left her last twenty dollars with a thank you note for the cleaning people and stopped by the cabin manager's office to express her appreciation. She exchanged addresses with Jennifer, who urged her to remember her dream from the first night and "write it down!"

Liz had a little surge of joy at the thought of writing again and found herself eager to start. She had almost forgotten what that felt like, but before the wheels of the plane had folded up, she was scribbling words as fast as she could onto the back pages of her journal.

[Ironically, a month later she saw an ad for a short story writing contest in a Christian magazine. Since the theme was "spiritual warfare," she sent the story in, not with any illusions of winning, but simply to make a point. To no one's surprise, it didn't win or place or get honorable mention. In fact, it was never acknowledged that it had been received.]

There was an assortment of people waiting at baggage claim when Liz got to Chicago, but she found Sean easily enough; he was the one with the Jesus t-shirt. He greeted her with a bear hug that lingered as if to make up for their time apart.

"So, Guitar Lady, how was the trip?" he asked, taking her carry-on bag and guitar.

"It was … very enlightening," Liz admitted, betraying mixed emotions.

"So you told me. Anything specific I should know about?"

"Well, I doubt I'm going to be a famous songwriter…"

"Hey, don't give up so easily. This was just your first try."

"OK, I'm *probably* not going to be a famous songwriter any time soon, maybe never, but that's OK, the operative word was 'famous.' So few people reach that place, and I'm not sure I'd even want it after what I've seen. I'm not sure I could handle it."

"It's definitely no place for a baby Christian, or most not-so-baby Christians, for that matter," Sean agreed. "All the pressures, temptations, distractions … pretty scary stuff. Maybe that's why the Lord doesn't let many of His kids get that far."

"Well, there sure are a lot that *want* to, anyway. And a lot were crushed and disappointed this week. I've never *seen* so many depressed Christians all in one place before!"

"Maybe that's not such a bad thing, depending on what you do with the experience… Is that your bag? I'll get it." He arranged the small bag on top of the larger one, pulled the handle out for dragging, and took her guitar in his other hand. Liz walked with him, carrying just her purse; it felt good to have someone else take her burdens. "We all need our egos brought down a notch every now and then," he went on. "Now the question is, are you going to get depressed and give up, or…”

“…look for other ways to serve Him? I did, and—Oh Sean, I have so much to tell you!”

“Well, you've got three days to do it.”

Liz was struck by the sheer vastness of the Chicago area. She had been aware that it was bigger than St, Louis, but she had spent most of her childhood in the vicinity of Clayton and Ladue and probably had not really considered the large size of her own home town, much less this major metropolis. Ironically, although she had visited Paris, London, and Rome, she had seen Chicago only through the window of an airplane when she had stopped there a few times to change flights. Now she was riding with Sean through the suburbs, each neighborhood having its own personality. She stared out the window, watching anxiously for a house that fit Sean's description of his home and taking in everything she saw, sensing somehow that all of this could be an important part of her life in the near future.

She felt a flutter in her stomach as Sean pointed to a quaint house nestled among some oak trees; as far as she could remember, she had never been brought home to “meet the parents” before.

“Wait'll you see the inside,” Sean warned. “You'll think you're in a time warp—or a weekend trip to Ireland.” Since Liz had never been to Ireland, she wasn't sure what that meant, but she could see through the lace curtains that someone was approaching; she'd find out soon enough. After some clicking of the latch there was a little jerk of the door as it opened, and there stood a petit, middle-aged woman with curly red hair, a ruddy complexion, and sparkling green eyes. She had on an apron over a simple cotton sundress. At the sight of her son, her round face broke into a broad, dimpled smile.

“Hey, Mom,” Sean greeted her.

“Shahnee!” she cried, giving him a big hug. “And this sweet thing must be Elizabeth! Do come in!” she said, taking both of Liz's hands in hers.

“Yes, it's nice to meet you,” Liz replied, feeling her shyness quickly leaving. “You can call me Liz.”

“What a pleasure to meet you, dear!” Mrs. O'Brien's musical voice had slightly Irish dialect, and as they stepped into the living room, Liz saw that the décor of the home had a similar accent. There was definitely an authentic Irish touch, yet contrary to what Sean had said, it did not look like stage scenery; it was just Irish enough to show some individuality. The smell of lamb was in the air, and Liz became suddenly aware of how hungry she was.

"Michael! Shannon!" Mrs. O'Brien called. "Turn off the video games! Sean's here with his lady friend!" Liz blushed at the title, and Sean chuckled, giving her hand a squeeze.

Two teenagers—obviously siblings—appeared in the doorway from the den. The boy, about eighteen, bore a striking resemblance to Sean, except that his hair was redder and longer, and his jeans baggier. The girl, about sixteen, had the same Irish features as her mother, and a fresh face that communicated friendliness and optimism. She wore faded jeans and a maroon T-shirt that said, "God isn't dead, I just talked to Him this morning."

"So you must be Katie!" exclaimed Michael, turning to Liz. "Sean's told us all about you. In fact, you're all he talks about. 'Katie this, Katie that,'—He's just crazy about you…You are Katie, aren't you?" Liz glanced at Sean for a clue as to how to respond; Sean was rolling his eyes.

"Now Michael, don't be teasin' the girl," scolded his mother. "She just got here."

"Yeah, Mike, go comb your hair or something," said the girl, pushing him out of the way. "I'm Shannon," she added, taking Liz's hands the same way her mother had. "Oh, I like your ring!"

"Thanks," said Liz. "I've had it forever."

"Silver?"

"Yeah."

"And it's tarnished again," scolded Sean, pulling the rag from his pocket. "Give it here." Liz took off the ring and handed it to him, and he polished it as he talked. "Shannon plays the guitar, too," he said to Liz, then to Shannon, "And she sings alto, so I bet you two could do some good duets."

"Don't forget me!" Mike protested. "I play the spoons," he told Liz with a flirtatious wink.

"I'm sure she's impressed," Sean assured him. "Actually, Liz, my brother's tone deaf, but he's studying journalism, so hopefully he'll be able to live a somewhat meaningful life anyway."

"You're a writer?" Liz asked, genuinely interested.

"Not yet. I'm more of a read-and-react-er. The only things of mine published so far are my letters to the editor," he added with a smirk.

"Your father's not home yet, Shahnee," his mother said apologetically. "Probably held up in traffic again. That construction is everywhere now. In the meantime, why don't you take Lizzie's bag up and show her to her room?"

"Sounds like a plan to me," Sean replied agreeably. "C'mon Lizzie."

As Liz followed him up the narrow stairway, she could hear Mrs. O'Brien's voice ordering with a hint of Irish brogue, "And you two set the table. I've been cookin' all afternoon, so ye can make yersilves useful!'

"I like your family," Liz laughed as Sean laid her suitcase on the chair in the guest room.

"Yeah, they'll do," he said with a smile and a wink. "Just don't take Mike personally, though. He likes to tease people. Just know that the more he insults you, the more he likes you."

"I'll try to remember that."

When Liz came downstairs, the table was set with a lace tablecloth, candles, fine china, and Irish crystal goblets. A leg of lamb was prominently displayed, surrounded by small red potatoes, carrots, and peas.

"Gee, Mom," Mike complained. "Did you forget to buy hot dogs again?"

"Quit yer complainin', young man, and light the candles," his mother ordered, handing him the matches. "Then go put on a belt if you must wear those pants. You know how your father is about that."

"You mean how *you* are about that. Dad doesn't mind."

"Somebody mention my name?" A tall, blond man showed up just in time to change the subject. He smiled broadly as he looked at Liz, then at Sean.

"Oh—! Dad, this is Liz. Liz, this is my Dad," said Sean.

"Nice to meet you, Mr.—Reverend—?" Liz looked to Sean for help as she extended her hand.

"Call me 'Dan,'" the man replied, giving her a hearty handshake.

"And you may call me Colleen," said his wife.

"Not that anyone's asking," added Mike, glad to see that his mother had apparently forgotten the belt idea so quickly.

"You! Sit!" she snapped, not quite succeeding in keeping a stern expression. "…The rest of you may be seated as well," she added with a smile.

"This looks wonderful," Liz commented as they all took their seats.

"Looks can be deceiving," said Mike cryptically, dodging a smack from his mother.

"Ah, smell those rolls!" breathed Sean. "Liz, wait'll you taste Mom's rolls, they're the best."

"Thank you, Shahnee," his mother replied, smiling fondly at him while shooting a warning glance at her other son.

"They're not exactly on my diet, Mom," Shannon lamented.

"Give up on the diet, Sis," advised Mike. "Some people were just born to be pudgy." He gave her ribs a poke, and she jumped.

"Cut it out! I'll have you know, I've lost five pounds!" she bragged.

"Well look behind you, I think you'll find them," he shot back. Shannon's mouth dropped open in speechless outrage; actually it was clear that she was struggling to keep from laughing.

"Enough!" their father cut in. "Time to say grace." The family joined hands. Shannon kicked Mike under the table; both stifled a snicker. Liz shyly took Sean's hand on one side and Mike's on the other. What followed was a far cry from the sing-song little verse Liz had recited at meals all her life. Dan was talking to his Father and was certain that He was hearing every word. *And that's the way it should be,* she thought, even as Mike was starting up a thumb-war with her and avoiding the reproachful look his mother was giving him.

During both the prayer and the dinner conversation Liz began to see why Sean was the way he was. He had grown up in a home where the presence of God was a daily reality, not just Sunday mornings but moment by moment. He was there in the hard times, she knew that. But she could see that in this family, more often than not, He was there to bring warmth, pleasure, love, and laughter—everything that makes life worth living. It was a reality she was still only beginning to grasp. And while this family took God very seriously, they had a refreshingly lighthearted outlook on everything else, especially themselves.

"Great dinner, Mom. But you *will* remember the hot dogs tomorrow, right?"

"Go put on a belt, Michael."

This seemed like a good place to get used to the idea of a Christ-centered home. Liz would spend a great deal of time the rest of that summer traveling back and forth between St. Louis and Chicago, getting to know the O'Briens and hearing many of the colorful stories that made up their family history.

There was "Pastor Dan," whom the church had hired for his knack for one-on-one relating to the adolescent crowd. The strategy: get a young person "turned onto Jesus" so much that he would invite a friend to church, who would likewise get excited and bring his family and more friends. Since Faith Chapel's vision was "to make God famous," Pastor Dan fit right in. Now that he had "graduated" into doing adult ministry, he was still serving many of the not-quite-as-young people he had met years before.

There was Sean's mother, Colleen, born and raised in Ireland, whose Irish brogue came out when she was angry, warning, or giving orders. (As a mother of three, this could be pretty frequent.)

Michael, the outspoken politician, knew more about current events on any given day than the rest of the family put together and had a definite opinion about everything. He loved a good debate, wrote letters to the editor, and even called radio talk shows to air his convictions. One would never guess that he was a staunch conservative from the "casual" way he dressed. Liz didn't know if this was because he could better relate to "the other side" if he wasn't dressed in a three-piece suit, or if he just liked to catch people off guard and keep them wondering.

Little sister Shannon was an easy-going sixteen-year-old, refreshingly free of the neuroses of many girls her age. Liz admired, even envied her confidence and the fact that she didn't waste time trying to be something she wasn't or wanting to be liked by everybody. (Shannon figured she would never have time to be everyone's friend anyway.) As it was, there were plenty of her peers who liked her, and she had become somewhat of a leader and role model, though she had never consciously tried to be.

There were more O'Brien relatives that Liz would eventually meet, some whose reputations preceded them, but this was Sean's immediate family, and Liz soon felt what a blessing it was to know them—a blessing well worth the price she had paid. She thought back to the time when the Lord had made it clear to her that she was not to stay emotionally involved with Aaron, although he had seemed like a decent person, who was extremely good-looking, and who had adored her. At the time it had seemed cruel to Liz to have to break up with him just because he wasn't a Christian and had no intention of ever becoming one; on the other hand, she had to ask herself, what good is a faith that quits as soon as things get hard? She was glad now that she had made the right choice; a handsome face was certainly no replacement for a relationship with her Creator, who would heal her broken heart eventually.

Now she realized that God had healed her more quickly than she would ever have hoped, and she was forever grateful. And the more she grew to love that blue-eyed, freckled face and his adoring smile, the more beautiful he was to her. Now, as she got to know Sean's family, she could see more and more clearly how God had been looking out for her, sending her not only a man who gave her the Christ-centered love she needed, but a family that would love her as well. She knew nothing about Aaron's family, but she doubted that they could ever have given her as much joy as Sean's.

If only all of life's trials could be resolved so neatly.

"Everyone ready?" asked Pastor Dan as the family gathered at the front door.

"Almost everyone," Sean laughed.

"Yo, Shannon!" yelled Mike. "Put down the curling iron and move your—"

"Coming!" Shannon sang, bounding down the stairs and out the door. The rest followed and piled into the car.

Liz wasn't sure what to expect. She had never gone to church on a Wednesday night before, and the only other churches she had been to were the one she had grown up in and the one she had attended the last few Sundays of her senior year at the University, which were different as caviar and peanut butter. (She preferred peanut butter.) She hadn't been involved in the youth group growing up, as she was shy and didn't know how to break into the groups of friends who attended different schools from hers. The kids in the group that she had known were the same ones that had teased her at the country club pool all summer, no doubt contributing to her negative body image, so even though she had been grateful for more structure (and clothes) at church, still her feeling had been pretty much "been there, suffered that." She had passed on the youth group's bowling and skating, and as for Sunday mornings, as bored as she was attending church with her parents, she had preferred it to Sunday school with the youth, for the same reasons. Finally, she had found a way to avoid both by volunteering to care for the babies in the nursery. Playing with the babies had been a way to pass the time, but she had received very little insights or revelations from playing "Patty-Cake."

It had never occurred to her that the answers to her fears and feelings of emptiness might be found in the messages given in the services or classes. Like the babies she cared for, she had never focused in the right direction long enough to find out.

Then there was Intervarsity, the fellowship at the university. She had finally decided to give it a try at the end of her senior year, after her unusual dreams and the persistence of a Christian roommate, Sarah, had brought her face-to-face with the Living God. "I.V." had been so different from anything she had known, so open and warm and genuine and powerful. Whether the difference was in the meetings or in herself, she found the antithesis to her old church experiences; she now could sing the songs wholeheartedly and grab hold of the messages like a drowning man grabbing a lifeline. She had kicked herself for waiting so long to accept Sarah's invitations. As soon as she had grown accustomed to (or addicted to) those gatherings, she had graduated and left the university town. She had a personal relationship with God now, which made all the difference, but she still missed I.V. and doubted that there would be another experience like it, at least not this side of heaven.

Tonight she was headed for yet another church experience, and since she liked Sean's family so much already, she had positive expectations about going where they worshipped.

"Wednesday nights aren't exactly family time for us," Sean's mom explained to Liz as they pulled into the church parking lot. "Dan and I will be goin' to the regular adult Bible study. He alternates with the other pastors and teaches about once a month. Mike's goin' to the college and career group, Shannon's goin' to the youth group, and Sean … well," she laughed, "I guess he's not usually here. Where will you be goin' tonight, dear?"

"He may as well come to youth group," Shannon interrupted, hopping out of the car, " 'cause that's where Liz is going."

"I am?" Liz smiled, stepping out.

"Actually, I was thinking about sitting in on them tonight," Sean said. Then detecting a twinge of disappointment in his father's face, he added, "unless you're teaching tonight, Dad."

"Actually, it's Pastor Duane's turn tonight," his father said, obviously appreciating Sean's asking.

"Sean's never quite left high school in his heart," his mother told Liz. "He's probably shared with you about getting into youth work starting this fall."

"Sort of…" Liz said hesitantly. "He's mentioned drama ministry."

"I'll be doing both," Sean explained. "Seems when you have a drama project it's usually the youth that get the most excited about it."

"True," agreed Pastor Dan. "Seems when most people get older they're not as apt to volunteer to be in the spotlight. I don't know if it's modesty, busyness, or laziness, but if you're going to do drama, it's best to open it up to the young people."

"'Cause we're so hungry for attention," Shannon whined, sticking out her lower lip.

"You poor little thing," said Mike. "You'd better get yourself some talent, then."

"And I suppose you're the next Johnny Depp? C'mon, Liz, I'll introduce you to everyone."

"Uh, mind if I come with you?" asked Sean facetiously.

"Sure, I suppose," said Shannon, ignoring his sarcasm.

Liz was delighted to hear the sound of a live band as they headed down the hall, and she hoped it was coming from the room where they were headed; it was. Shannon led the way into a room that was large, but apparently not large enough. Teens were gathering in the back as youth workers scrambled to set up more chairs. Many of the kids reminded Liz of I.V. Cut-offs and t-shirts were the norm, although there was a occasional "Goth" or "prep," and a few of them had pants big enough to smuggle illegal aliens. Liz was pleased to see that there didn't seem to be any harassment or rejection going on. The kids talked loudly in small clusters, and a few guys and one lanky girl were shooting baskets until the workers told them apologetically that they'd have to move to make room for more chairs. The kids put the ball back on the shelf and agreeably grabbed some chairs to set up. Shannon was greeted by almost everybody, and a few recognized Sean and welcomed him back. Sean and Shannon were both quick to introduce Liz, but between the band's playing and the sheer number of kids she met, Liz doubted that she would be able to recall many of the names.

Soon the band stopped, and the leader came to the microphone and asked everyone to find a seat. He apologized for the shortage of chairs, but it was obvious to everyone that he was delighted to have this kind of "problem," especially since, as he pointed out, a new facility was being built that would soon afford much more room for this ministry. As the O'Briens had explained to Liz, Faith Chapel had gone from one Sunday morning service to two and was soon to add an "early bird" service. ("And you don't want to know what time *that* starts!" Shannon had told Liz.) Still, the church seemed to be splitting at the seams, and everyone was looking forward to the grand opening of their new facility, a mammoth structure that was in the final stages of being built.

"Now that you're all sitting," the leader announced with a smile, "let's stand for praise and worship." The kids stood noisily as the drummer did an intro and the guitar and keyboard joined in. Lyrics were projected on the overhead screen, like the ones

Liz had sung from at I.V., except more "high tech." These had photos or moving patterns behind them that seemed to go with each song: a rushing stream, stars spinning through the universe, a worshipper with outstretched arms.

The youth sang, some with gusto, some clapping, some jumping up and down, some just concentrating on reading the lyrics. Liz thought of her own teenaged years, so lost and empty, and envied these kids. If only something like this had been available to her when she was this age… Then she reminded herself that she was here to focus on God, not on the kids, the pictures, or her own regrets. She closed her eyes, abandoned the self-pity, and poured out her praise with the others. Moments later she was swept up in a feeling she recognized gladly—the worship that swelled in that room, the very presence of God.

The rest of the meeting went much like an I.V. gathering, except without the brief but profound skits Sean and a few others had performed each week. Liz missed them. As the worship leader closed the prayer and the youth pastor took over the microphone to give the message, Liz whispered to Sean, "They need a drama team."

Sean just smiled.

Two days later Liz and Sean were standing at the front door of Liz's home in the St. Louis suburb of Ladue. Liz was glad Sean's ministry training was flexible enough that he could come to St. Louis for a few days. The sun was finally dipping behind the tall oaks, bringing a reprieve from the August heat.

"Nice neighborhood," Sean commented, looking around at the large brick houses, gardens, and well manicured lawns. The voices of children playing blended with the rhythmic hissing of the sprinkler system next door, and a young couple trotted by in stylish jogging suits.

"Hey, Lah-dee-doo's the best," Liz laughed.

As the door opened, they were face to face with someone who clearly didn't fit the "Lah-dee-doo" stereotype. Sean tried not to look startled at the sight of a freckled face with no makeup, Bohemian style skirt and blouse, and the brightly colored scarf tied around the chestnut hair that was otherwise wild and free. Liz's jaw dropped in astonishment.

"Elaine!" she gasped.

"Hey, sis!" The freckled face broke into a broad smile. "Surprise!" The sisters hugged so enthusiastically that Liz almost fell over.

"What are you doing here?" she asked, still breathless.

"Well, I heard you were out west for a whole week—and *didn't bother to come see me,*" she added with as much outrage as she could muster. "So, I thought I'd better come see you."

"I was in Colorado, Elaine. That's not exactly around the corner from San Francisco."

"Excuses, excuses. Anyway, I was thinking I was due for a visit to Mom and Dad anyway, then I heard you had this hot dude you wanted to introduce to them. Didn't want to miss out on *that*." Elaine's teasing had the desired effect, and Liz's face turned a noticeable shade of pink. "So, you gonna introduce me to him or not?"

"Uh, Elaine, this is Sean. Sean, my sister Elaine."

"Liz has told me all about you," Sean smiled.

"Really?" Elaine cast a sideways glance at her sister. "I'd be interested to hear her version of the story one of these days." Then turning suddenly, she yelled up the stairs, "MOM! DAD! Liz and her honey are here!"

"Good grief, Elaine!" Liz groaned.

"So how long are you here for?" Sean asked.

" 'til Tuesday. Our group has a meeting Tuesday night I don't want to miss. And," she added to Liz, " you know how helpless Rick is with me gone. Last time he did the laundry the sheets came out pink."

Just then a suntanned man appeared at the kitchen door wearing a golf shirt and shorts.

"Liz! Honey! I didn't hear you pull up!" He gave Liz a hearty hug and kiss.

"Hey, Dad!" said Liz, hugging him. Just then another voice came from upstairs.

"Is that Elizabeth?"

"Yes, dear," George called back. Turning to Liz, he grinned and said, "I see you found out about the surprise."

"Yes! I can't believe Elaine's here! This is great!"

"Elizabeth!" A forty-something woman in a tennis dress came down the stairs.

"Mom!" Liz went to hug her mother, but Rachel was hesitant.

"Oh honey, I'm all sticky from playing tennis. I *just* got back."

"Don't worry about it," Liz said, hugging her anyway. "Mom, this is Sean. Sean, my mother."

"I apologize, I was hoping to clean up before…"

"Not a problem," Sean assured her. "I like tennis, too."

"We'll have to get up some doubles," George suggested.

"There's five of us, Dad," Elaine pointed out, then added with a fiendish gleam in her eye, "It'll have to be … *Round Robin!*"

"I'm not sure I'd be up to *that*," Rachel gasped. What she meant was actually that she would be mortified if any of her family were to be seen on the country club tennis courts indulging in Uncle-Jack-type craziness.

"So, what is this 'Round Robin'?" Sean wanted to know.

"Our family's version probably isn't like any 'Round Robin' you've ever seen," Elaine warned.

"Our cousins taught it to us one Christmas when we were playing ping-pong," said Liz. "You divide the people into two groups and have them at separate ends of the table, lined up to hit the ball. Once you've hit it, the person behind you gets the next one. You have to run to the line on the other side of the table and wait your turn to hit it again."

"Only the 'line' keeps getting shorter," Elaine broke in. "Because every time someone misses it, that person is out. Pretty soon there are just a few people running around the table."

"And by the time there are just three people, they're *really* tearing around," Liz added.

"And when one of them gets out…?"

"Then you just play a regular point to see who the winner is."

"Sounds like fun!" said Sean.

"Of course, when summer came and we translated that to a tennis court…!" Elaine began.

"We get a *real* workout!"

"Or a heart attack."

"I can imagine," said Sean. "From what I've heard about your cousins, that sounds just like something they'd do."

"So Liz has told you our family's crazy?" Elaine guessed.

"Elaine!" Rachel protested.

"Hey, it's a good thing!" Elaine assured her. George decided to change the subject.

"Liz, would you like to take Sean up to the guest room?" he suggested.

"Sure," Liz agreed, picking up her guitar and leading the way. Grabbing both bags for balance, Sean followed her upstairs.

"I like your family," Sean said to Liz as she showed him the guest room.

"Yeah, they'll do," Liz mimicked, sensing the déjà vu.

"So when are we going to the Arch?"

"The Arch?"

"Yeah, this is St. Louis, isn't it?"

"Yeah, I just never thought of doing that… I mean, good idea! I'd like to."

"You've never been up in the Arch before, have you?"

"Um…no."

"But you live here, Liz!"

"I know. I just haven't gotten around to it…"

"Let me get this straight. You've been up in the Eiffel Tower but not the St. Louis Arch?"

"Yep. And when was the last time you went up in the Sears Tower, Chicago Boy?"

"Touché."

The tourists at the Arch came in all colors, sizes, and styles, so a family consisting of two country-clubbers, two recent college grads, and one free spirit went virtually unnoticed. While George and Rachel made their way to the entrance, Sean stopped to give a word of encouragement and a high-five to a young boy wearing a Christian t-shirt, and Elaine stopped to snap pictures of the Arch from unique angles that wouldn't have occurred to most people.

"Are you guys coming?" Liz called, not wanting to lose her parents.

After moving at a snail's pace through a tight line, the group was packed into a pod that transported them to the top of the Arch, pausing several times along the way to rotate with an unnerving jerk so the passengers wouldn't arrive at the top sideways. It was the kind of close quarters that reminds one of sardines, and Sean, noticing the look on Rachel's face, perceived that she was a bit claustrophobic. The space at the top where the tourists could look out wasn't much larger, but the view was magnificent. It was a clear day, so one could see the whole city and beyond. Elaine snapped pictures with her telephoto lens, and George persuaded a stranger to take a family picture so Elaine could be in it. Rachel, who was more reserved with strangers, protested to him privately, but George wasn't concerned about the camera.

"He's not going to make off with it," he reasoned, not quite in a whisper. "Where could he go?" Rachel hissed in his ear that that wasn't what she meant. (The family portrait turned out well, except Rachel's face was a little redder than everyone else's.)

When they were back on the ground and had traced the journey of Lewis and Clark and bought a postcard for Sean's family, George invited everyone to lunch at the country club.

"How about someplace *different?*" Elaine suggested. "St. Louis has a million restaurants."

"But Sean's never seen the country club," George reasoned.

"He's never seen any of the other million restaurants, either," Elaine argued. She looked at Sean for some kind of support.

"Um, either is fine with me," he said, not wanting to be in the middle of a family disagreement.

"The country club it is," George concluded happily, starting up the car.

"Same-old-same-old," Elaine muttered under her breath.

Upon arriving, they were politely turned away at the door, the maitre d' explaining apologetically that "blue jeans" were not permitted in the dining room. As Sean was the only one wearing the offending garment, Liz's immediate instinct was to protect her beloved from humiliation. Her reaction was uncharacteristically defiant, though characteristically she waited until she was out of earshot of the maitre d'.

"Well aren't we high and mighty?" she fretted as they headed for the door. "Jeans are *normal* these days. They need to lighten up and get their heads out of the nineteenth century!"

"Liz!" exclaimed Elaine, surprised at her sister's outburst.

Sean took Liz's hand. "*Who* needs to lighten up?" he rebuked her gently.

George dealt with the situation with his usual humor. "We'll just take our business elsewhere!" he declared with mock outrage. Rachel shushed him, and Elaine laughed. Liz was still indignant.

"Good grief, what is their *problem?*" she griped. Then cracking a smile in spite of herself, she added, "Elaine looks way weirder than Sean!"

"Gee, thanks, sis," said Elaine brightly.

Once they were outside, Sean began to apologize to Liz's parents, but Rachel was quick to take the blame.

"We didn't even *think* about the dress code," she sighed, "and there's certainly no way *you* could have known."

Liz then began to worry that what was meant to be gracious could come across as condescending and only make things worse. She felt slightly sick.

But as they were walking past the golf course, Elaine, whose motto in life seemed to be "Lighten up," was saying something to Sean that made him smirk. Elaine was chuckling and smiling at Liz as if trying to share a private joke.

"What's so funny?" she asked Sean when her parents were out of earshot.

"Your sister was just pointing out the 'proper' way to dress at this establishment," he explained, nodding in the direction of a group of elderly golfers. The garish outfits sported by these apparently colorblind weekend warriors were more than one could look at with a straight face. Liz practically laughed out loud, both with amusement and relief that Sean seemed to be having a good time, "blue jeans" and all.

Elaine proceeded to tell the others about a great out-of-the-way place she had discovered last time she had visited St. Louis and suggested they all go there. Rachel was a little dubious about going to an unfamiliar neighborhood. However, she was first and foremost a gracious hostess, wanting to make her guest more comfortable as soon as possible. "Why not?" she responded.

It was an exotic lunch that day, surrounded by an assembly of "artsy" types. Now it was Liz's parents' turn to be slightly out of place, but no one except the insecure Liz seemed to think anything of it. As the meal progressed, she was pleasantly surprised at her parents' adaptability. They were treated to some unusual experiences (unusual to everyone but Elaine) such as dishes containing goat's cheese, grains Liz had never heard of, and vegetarian anything one could imagine—all natural, of course, with no preservatives. George grumbled good-naturedly that at his age he needed all the preservatives he could get, but nevertheless he finished every bite. Rachel, who wasn't used to this much novelty without being accompanied by a tour guide, actually seemed to be enjoying the adventure by the time dessert arrived.

"This reminds me of something we had in Thailand," she commented. "Honey, do you remember that coconut soup we had in Bangkok?"

"What a memory your mother has!" George laughed heartily. "We spent three weeks touring the Far East, and she remembers coconut soup in Bangkok!"

"Three weeks? What countries did you see?" Sean wanted to know.

That was all George and Rachel needed to hear. If there had been any remaining awkwardness, it melted away at that moment. The couple became suddenly animated, recounting their journeys abroad until Elaine and Liz resorted to playing Hangman on their napkins to entertain themselves. Liz prayed that the interested expression on Sean's face was sincere as he heard all about adventures in the Far East, an African safari, a Mediterranean cruise, and an excursion to the Arctic. (It became quite obvious that George and Rachel had not wasted any time grieving over their empty nest.) Finally George commented, "I think they're going to kick us out of here if we don't leave soon."

"Good heavens!" Rachel declared, looking at her watch. "It's after three o'clock!"

"Time flies when you're having fun," Liz grinned, stuffing the Hangman napkin in her pocket.

"Yeah, now wasn't this place a lot more interesting than the same-old-same-old at the no-jeans-allowed club?"

"Well, Elaine, I'm not sure I'd put it *that* way," George chuckled. "It was *different*, but you know we love the club." (What he really meant, of course, was that he loved being able to show off his family to his friends.)

"But a change is nice now and then," Rachel added.

"And *Sean* made it all possible!" Elaine declared.

*Geez, don't embarrass him **again**!* Liz fretted to herself.

But Sean took it well and said modestly, "My pleasure."

"Your parents are cool," Sean told Liz later.

"You think?" Liz asked. She had been afraid that the country club lifestyle and awkward situations had ruined his first impression of her family. "I mean, I love 'em to pieces, but I'm not sure I've ever thought of them as 'cool'."

"Well I would. I loved hearing about all their travels. It sounds like they've been just about everywhere."

"Yeah, they do like to see new places. Just don't ask to see my dad's pictures. He has a million of them."

Sean smirked. "You don't like slide shows?"

"Actually, it's pretty funny when they start showing pictures. They've been so many places they start to get mixed up, and Dad'll say it's a picture of Windsor Castle, and Mom'll swear it's someplace else."

"Well, it's still cool that they've traveled the world together."

"Yeah, and it's ironic that when they're here the only places they want to go to are the country club and the M.A.C."

"M.A.C.?"

"Missouri Athletic Club."

"Oh."

"By the way, thanks for wearing the jeans today. Elaine and I always wanted to take Mom and Dad someplace new, and today you made it happen!"

"Hey, I aim to please," Sean chuckled. "Anyway, your parents were really good sports about it, especially your mom. You could tell she was uncomfortable more than once today—going up the Arch and eating health-nut cuisine, but she never tried to change what we were doing, she just made the best of it."

"You know, I think she was actually having a good time," said Liz.

"I think she just *decided* to, and she did."

"You're right. That *is* pretty … cool." Liz smiled as she realized she had one more reason to appreciate her mother.

And Sean.

Tuesday morning when Liz came downstairs she was surprised to see Sean in the big easy chair in the living room with a large photo album on his lap and a peculiar expression on his face.

"Hey, whatcha lookin' at?" she asked, coming over and sitting on the arm of the chair. "Oh my gosh! I haven't seen these in years! Where did you get this?"

Sean didn't seem to hear but continued to leaf through page after page of snapshots of Liz's parents and a young adolescent girl seeing the sights in Europe. The young girl had auburn hair and freckles and a camera around her neck.

"Man, was I pudgy back then!" she exclaimed. Again Sean didn't seem to have heard her.

"You never told me you'd been to Europe with your parents," he said in a tone that was difficult to interpret.

"Just once. It was the year Elaine spent the summer in Switzerland."

"Oh…" Sean seemed to be in another world himself as the turning pages showed young Liz feeding pigeons in front of the Louvre, pretending to hold up the Leaning Tower of Pisa, and standing at attention by a guard at Buckingham Palace. "What countries did you visit?" he asked.

"England, Germany, France, Italy … you know, the usual stuff. And Switzerland of course."

"To see Elaine."

"Yeah, we hiked around the Alps with her friends. It was great."

"Must've been. And you've been a few other places," he added, nodding toward the albums that were on the floor.

"Yeah, we always seemed to wind up somewhere in the Caribbean for spring break."

Sean said nothing, and Liz thought he seemed quieter than usual.

"Do you need a cup of coffee?" she asked as she headed for the kitchen.

"No thanks. I think I'll go for a run."

"Oh…OK." *Maybe that'll wake him up,* she thought. There was something in the air that made her uneasy, but she hoped it was nothing and that when Sean came back he'd be his old self and they'd have another great day.

"Hey, Sleeping Beauty!" came Elaine's perky voice. She was up and dressed already, even though it was two hours earlier in California. "Finally waking up, I see."

"Yeah, I'm getting lazy in my old age." Liz poured herself a cup of coffee.

"Sean's been up a while," said Elaine. "He seemed bored, so I showed him where the photo albums were."

"Yeah, I noticed. Thanks for showing him my fat pictures!" Liz got the milk out of the refrigerator and poured some into her coffee.

"You're welcome. I wouldn't worry about it, Liz, he's obviously crazy about you!" Liz smiled dreamily as she stirred her coffee. "I think you're a little crazy about him, too. Am I right?" Liz's smile broadened, and her cheeks flushed.

"Yeah, I think this might be the Real Thing," she confessed.

"Well, it's *about time* my little virgin sister's getting with the program!"

Liz's spoon fell to the floor with a clatter.

"Excuse me?!"

"You know. You've always done things all prim and proper like Mom and Dad like it. Even now, with the guest room and all. Doesn't it seem strange, you two sleeping in separate rooms?" Liz was speechless for a moment.

"Elaine, we don't live together. In fact, we've never …" Liz's face was beet red by now as she retrieved the spoon.

"You haven't—You've got to be kidding! And you're *how* old?"

"It isn't a matter of how old we are—or even what Mom and Dad want. It's a matter of … our faith." Liz hadn't known when she'd be getting around to sharing her faith with her family members, but apparently this might be the moment. "Sean and I are both Christians, so we want to do things … the way God wants us to."

Elaine looked at her as though she were from Mars.

"So you don't think God wants you enjoying each other?" she asked incredulously.

"No, we don't believe *that*…"

"So what does He have against you two expressing your love?"

"Nothing. There's just … more than one way to express love. Sometimes abstinence expresses it better than ... not abstaining."

"Really." Elaine remarked. "Explain." She leaned against the counter, looked at Liz expectantly, and chuckled, "This oughta be good."

Suddenly intimidated, Liz searched her groggy mind for the right words. "Well, if you really love someone, you want the best for them…" *Lord, help!* "We believe God loves us and wants the best for us, so if we do things God's way, that's what'll be … best for us…" *Real eloquent, Liz.*

"And His way is to be a prude?"

Ouch! "No!—I mean, *yes!* I mean…" She took a deep breath. *Just say it.* "Sean and I both believe sex is for married people."

"Wow… I feel like I'm in a time warp… So, what if you're sexually incompatible? Wouldn't you want to find that out *before* you take the Big Step?"

Liz wasn't sure how to respond to this kind of "logic," but while she hesitated, Elaine continued to dispense her worldly wisdom.

"Besides, you need to get to know each other. I wouldn't want to get to my wedding night and not know what the heck I was doing."

"Well, if we're *both* inexperienced, we could learn together. Wouldn't that be even better?" The words were out of Liz's mouth almost before they occurred to her. Suddenly she recalled a conversation Sean had told her about that seemed relevant to the discussion.

"Sean's roommate felt the same way you do," she began. "He thought Sean was crazy for not wanting to be 'experienced' before getting married. He said 'Hey, I want to test drive a car before I buy it!'"

"So, what did Sean say?" asked Elaine, who thought the roommate had a good point.

Liz set down her cup and paused for emphasis, smiling at the thought of her "knight in shining armor."

"He just looked at him and said, *'My girlfriend is not a car.'* The guy shut up after that."

Elaine was quiet for a moment.

"That *was* pretty cool of him," she admitted. She smiled affectionately at her little sister. "Well, your way isn't for me, but I respect you for it."

"Thanks," said Liz, relieved that they hadn't got into an uncomfortable debate.

Just then Elaine's cell phone rang. She grabbed it out of her purse, checked the caller I.D., and excused herself. Liz could hear her on the patio saying, "Hi honey! Yep, I'll be home tonight. .. Not 'til 6:00. I have a layover in Denver. Can't wait to see you! Love ya!"

Sean came back from his run, breathless. Liz wanted to tell him about her conversation with Elaine and how much she appreciated him, but he just said, "I'm gonna hop in the shower," and disappeared abruptly. Liz was beginning to feel as though something was wrong; she was not used to his having so little to say to her.

The family saw Elaine off at the airport later that morning and then went to the country club to play a few sets of tennis. Sean did not seem particularly chatty, but then he had already been running, and the St. Louis humidity had a way of sucking the energy out of a person. It wasn't that Sean was playing poorly, but it seemed to Liz he was merely going through the motions.

As for Liz, she was having a hard time focusing herself. Tennis had never been a big deal for her to begin with. It was a pleasant enough diversion—as long as the weather was nice—and it was good exercise. But Liz had never pursued it as intensely as her sister had. Elaine was the family athlete. As a teenager she had played in rain, shine, or 110 degrees and humid, and she had the trophies to show for it. Liz wasn't about to try to compete with that, and she always had other things besides sports on her mind anyway. For her tennis had become something to do while she pondered and sorted out other things, and today was a prime example. While her eyes and reflexes focused on the little yellow ball, her mind was on Sean, trying to read what was wrong through his silence and searching through her memory for something she might have done to offend him.

"It's your serve, honey," George reminded her after she had hit the ball over to his side.

"Oh…I'm sorry. What's the score?"

Rachel returned the ball to her. "Cockadoodle-doo!" she teased.

Liz wondered how soon they'd be finished playing.

After tennis George and Rachel stayed at the club for a social event, and Liz and Sean grabbed a bite to eat and headed back to the house. Liz had been increasingly uneasy all day but had not wanted to ask any questions with her parents right there. Besides, she didn't really know what to ask. Sean was so silent and pensive in the car that Liz was close to tears.

After getting cleaned up from playing tennis, she found him sitting on the patio, staring at the yard. She was terrified of what she might find out if she confronted him, but she couldn't stand not knowing any longer. She pulled up a chair and sat down next to him.

"Talk to me," she said.

"'bout what?" he asked evasively.

"'bout why you've been so quiet today."

"Oh. I'm sorry. I've just been thinking."

"'bout what?" she mimicked, trying to ignore the knot in her stomach.

He sat quietly, watching the fountain, while Liz agonized over the possibility that her whole world could be blown apart any minute. The gurgling of the water and the familiar hissing of the sprinklers blended with the chirping of the crickets as she sat for what seemed like an hour, bracing herself for his answer. Finally he spoke.

"I don't know if I can be … if I can give you everything you want."

Everything I want? "What are you talking about?" Her heart was pounding. *Is he breaking up with me?*

"I'm talking about lifestyle. I'm never going to make the money your dad makes. Faith Chapel is a huge church, but that doesn't mean their staff is rolling in dough."

"Who ever said they were?" Liz was confused.

"Liz, I can't take you on trips to Europe or cruises to the Caribbean…"

"Did I ever say I expected you to?" *What kind of brat does he think I am?*

"No, but you're used to having … things … and I know you love to go places and see things and meet people…"

Liz knew better than to be dishonest with Sean.

"Sure I do," she admitted, "but there's more than one way to see the world," she added hastily.

"So you do want to see the world."

Liz hadn't expected this to be the topic of their heart-to-heart discussion, and being caught off guard, she didn't know quite what to say. But realizing now that it was Sean who needed reassuring, she wanted to be sure to say the right thing. She had done enough soul-searching and reflecting on the tennis court in times past to have come up with her philosophy of life, and her travels had already brought her to certain conclusions. She remembered a certain day playing tennis in Puerto Rico, acutely aware of the contrast between the resort and the slums she had seen earlier that day.

"Yes, I want to see the world, but not without a reason. Oh, it was fun for a while to look at the sights and take pictures, but I've also seen a lot of things I didn't like seeing, like poverty and ignorance. I decided long ago that if I ever go back to those places, I want to be part of the solution. Even as a kid when we were on vacation, after a while I'd start to ask myself, 'What am I here for?' And if I didn't have a good answer, I felt like it was time to go home."

"But if you end up with me, we might never *leave* home."

"Are you kidding? Where's your faith? If God calls us to go somewhere, we'll go wherever He sends us. I mean, other people go on mission trips all the time. We'll just have to write fundraising letters like everyone else."

Sean was silent for a moment. Finally Liz saw him crack a smile for the first time that day. "Well," he said, "we do know you've been called to write."

Liz felt a huge weight begin to be lifted. She felt relieved, but she also felt a little annoyed at what she'd been put through.

"You know, you *scared* me today!"

"I did? Sorry."

"I didn't know what was wrong. I was afraid … I was losing you." She felt the tears she'd held back all day start to well up.

"I can't see that happening, Liz."

"Really?"

Sean looked around at the house, the garden, the fountain, and the Mercedes in the driveway. "You may lose a lot of things, but I don't plan on being one of them."

"Well, neither do I," she said, taking his hand. He gave hers a squeeze. "Would you promise me something?" she asked, still feeling a little residual stress.

"What's that?"

"Next time something's bothering you, *talk* to me about it! Don't keep me guessing and *stressing* all day!" She gave him a shove.

Sean, who had already been leaning back in his chair, started to tip over. At the sight of his arms and legs flailing to try to regain his balance, Liz actually found herself stifling a laugh, but when the chair hit the pavement with Sean in it, she was suddenly concerned. She jumped out of her chair.

"Are you OK?" she asked, feeling a twinge of guilt. Sean seemed only a little startled. Dusting himself off, he rose shakily to his feet.

"OK, I deserved that," he said contritely. "I'm sorry." He opened his arms, and Liz accepted his offer of a hug. It felt so good to have him hold her again that Liz decided to let the whole thing go. They lingered in the peacefulness of the summer evening until the stress of the day finally subsided.

"Hey, you know when the day started going wrong?" Liz asked him when her mind was clear.

"Hmm… I'm not sure. When?"

"Probably at the very beginning. Did you pray this morning?"

"Uh… oops. No, I didn't. Elaine gave me that photo album, and I …"

"Well, I didn't either. BIG mistake. And look what happened to us."

"Yeah, we kinda wasted the whole day. Some kind of spiritual leader I'm turning out to be."

"Hey, isn't our faith all about starting over? Besides, the day's not over yet."

"Right. Better late than never." He took her hand again, and after apologizing to Jesus for leaving Him out, they committed their day—what was left of it—to Him.

"Hey, Sean?" Liz asked after they had said "amen." "Did you really think I wanted to spend my life luxuriating on a beach somewhere or running around being a tourist?"

"Now that I think of it, I can't see you doing that," he admitted.

"Elaine loves to do stuff like that, but I want to make a difference."

"Well, you've already made a difference to me."

"Besides, my attention span is so short …"

"Yeah, I noticed that today on the tennis court."

CHAPTER FOURTEEN

It wasn't long before Liz was back in Chicago, feeling at home in what the O'Briens had dubbed "Liz's room." She was feeling so much a part of Sean's family that Sean no longer hesitated to leave her with them to work at the church or go for his morning run.

The only person Liz found in the kitchen when she came downstairs that morning was Mike. Liz asked where Sean was, and as Mike replied "Running," and abruptly changed the subject to what he was reading in the paper, she had mixed feelings about getting into a discussion with him.

Since Mike made a point of knowing everything he could about what was going on in the world, talking to him could be very enlightening. It could also be humbling, even intimidating for someone like Liz, who rarely read or listened to the mainstream media, much less made the effort to find out what the mainstream media was leaving out. This was one of those mornings Mike was on his soapbox, and Liz was really hoping Sean would return soon from his daily run to rescue her from total humiliation.

There had been another terrorist attack in the Middle East, and by the time Liz had poured her first cup of coffee Mike was expounding on the conflict between Israel and Palestine and what the US should and shouldn't be doing about it.

For the past four years Liz's focus had been on school and theater and somehow graduating and being able to do something with her degree. The Middle East conflict had been to her something that was happening far from home and was much too complicated for her to sort out, even if she had had the time or felt the need to. Before college she had known even less about world affairs, being the stereotypical self-absorbed American teenager.

So here she sat in the O'Briens' kitchen, listening to Mike talk about Hamas and Al Quaida and someone named…*what was it … Ben Alladin?* Her head was swimming. She had been somewhat educated by Mike in the past but felt that this morning all this was way over her head. For a while she sat silently, sipping her coffee and listening to Mike's lecture about people and places that sounded vaguely familiar. When there was a lull in the speech, she finally spoke.

"I guess I haven't paid much attention to all that, since it doesn't seem to have much to do with where we live …" she said sheepishly, hoping Mike would dumb down the lesson a bit for her sake. The astonished look he gave her made her feel even more mortified by her ignorance.

"You think this has nothing to do with *us?*" he asked incredulously. "Haven't you been reading the news for the past seven years?"

"Watch it, Mike," warned his sister, who had just come in. "You've only been reading the papers for two years."

Thanks, Shannon! Liz thought.

Mike apologized, took a deep breath, and gave Liz her current events mini-lesson of the day.

"The US has been the victim of terrorist attacks all over the world—attacks on our military bases, our embassies, our diplomats kidnapped and murdered, hijackings …"

"Oh yeah, in other places…" Liz did remember hearing about those things briefly, but these things had seemed to disappear as soon as the news report was over. "It's just natural not to think about those things, since they don't happen right here … in America itself …" She was feeling more awkward by the minute. "…much…?" When she saw Mike brace himself for another speech, she decided that the best thing to do was just to keep quiet and wait for Sean to come back.

"February, 1993—that's just a little over seven years ago—Al Quaida attacked the World Trade Center with a car bomb." Although Liz had heard of the attack, she realized to her chagrin that she wasn't even sure where the World Trade Center was, but she wasn't about to let Mike know that.

"Oh yeah, *duh,* I forgot about that…"

"They only killed six people, but they injured a thousand," Mike went on, "and what they wanted to do was make one of the towers collapse, maybe even knock down the other. Can you imagine how many people would have died?!"

Liz had no idea, so all she said was, "Wow…"

"They found all these bomb-making manuals in the apartment of one of the attackers—all in Arabic, of course…"

"*Of course,*" added Shannon knowingly. Mike wasn't looking at her, so she made a mocking know-it-all face at him that made Liz stifle a smile and feel just a little less uncomfortable.

"One of the attackers was brought back to the U.S. from Pakistan. He said his only regret was not using more explosives… and he said they'd try again."

"'If at first you don't succeed…'" chirped Shannon.

"You think this is funny?!" Mike snapped, turning around. Shannon's eyes got big, her mouth clamped shut, and she grabbed a muffin and exited, leaving Liz the sole student once again.

"So, there *has* been an attack on U.S. soil …" she said soberly.

"More than one. That same year they arrested some conspirators that were planning *another* attack July Fourth. They had suicide bombers ready to target U.N. Headquarters and car bombs aimed at George Washington Bridge, Lincoln and Holland Tunnels, and the main office of the FBI!"

"Yikes!" exclaimed Liz. It wasn't very profound or educated-sounding, but "yikes" was all she could come up with at the moment. "And that was all seven years ago? Has there been anything here since then?"

"In '97 there were some letter bombs—"

"Oh yeah, I heard about those, too."

"—in some major cities, including Washington D.C. Then there was that Palestinian sniper that shot at tourists from the Empire State Building."

"Where do you learn all this stuff?" Liz asked.

"Internet, radio, newspapers …"

"I read the paper … sometimes… but I don't remember details like you do."

"That's because he spends hours at the computer every day," panted Sean, who had just come in from his run. His face was flushed, and he was dripping with sweat. Delighted (and relieved) to see him, Liz jumped up to get him a drink.

"We've been talking about Middle Eastern affairs and the threat of terrorism in America today," she explained, taking a glass from the cupboard with a look that said, "and I know *all* about those things, don't I?"

"So what do they want from us?" she asked, going to the freezer for some ice. She was finding all this very disturbing, and she had decided it was time to get to the bottom line.

"Mainly, they just hate us for being an ally of Israel, and they see us as interfering in Middle Eastern affairs."

Liz let that sink in as she filled the glass with water and handed it to Sean.

"The biggest disaster I can remember clearly had nothing to do with that," she said. "It was the Oklahoma City bombing about five years ago. That I remember real well."

"You're right, that had nothing to do with the Arab-Israeli thing," said Sean, "but I remember that was the first thing people thought of when it happened."

"I can see why now." Liz had learned a few things that morning, but she wasn't exactly thrilled at what she was learning. It was sobering stuff, and it made her think of the bigger picture, of things like evil and truth and God. And she began to wonder if it involved more than politics.

"It seems once about every two or three years something horrible happens—like Oklahoma City and Columbine—and people get real sober and spiritually minded … *for a while.*"

"Yeah, and church attendance goes up … *for a while* …" Sean knew exactly what she meant.

"It makes you wonder if we need these disasters to keep us from forgetting God," Liz thought out loud. "I mean, have you ever wondered what would happen if people stayed spiritual? Would the tragedies stop? What do you think?"

"I think we'll never know," Sean sighed. "Everybody always gets back to 'business as usual.'"

"Yeah," said Mike in disgust. "The usual complacent, ignorant, sheltered Americans, taking everything for granted. But we need to realize we're not as sheltered as we think we are, even if we don't live in New York or D.C. You know, one of those letter bombs in '97 ended up in Leavenworth Prison."

"That's in Kansas." Sean whispered, seeing Liz's puzzled expression.

"I was always terrible in geography. I feel so ignorant!" she moaned, slumping back into her chair.

"Hey, we're all ignorant, just in different subjects," Mike quipped, and Liz saw him smile for the first time that morning. Liz was relieved to see him lighten up.

"Well, I'm a little less ignorant this morning, thanks to you." Liz smiled back, and the gratified look on Mike's face told her he wasn't disgusted with her, just glad he could enlighten her.

"Hey Mike, don't you have to go listen to Rush or something?" Sean asked. Mike took the hint.

"Yeah, I'm gonna go hit the Internet for a while."

"Have … fun," said Liz. She turned to Sean and shrugged, not knowing if that had been an appropriate thing to say. Sean smiled and shook his head.

"So, you got to listen to my brother's speeches this morning?"

"Yeah, he's pretty interesting, actually. But today I think he was way over my head."

"He'd like us to think he is," Sean chuckled.

"Actually, I did learn some things, or maybe I was reminded of some things I shouldn't have forgotten."

"You mean like we're vulnerable? Life is uncertain? No one's promised tomorrow?"

"Well, when you put it that way, I guess that's old news. Yeah, we're all in the same boat, aren't we?"

"Actually, there are two boats. For us, if we don't survive tomorrow in this life, we have another, better life to look forward to. For others, if *they* die…"

"Either unexpectedly or on purpose…" Liz murmured, thinking of the suicide bombers.

"It's a different story," Sean finished the thought sadly.

"Is that like part of their religion or something?" Liz asked. "Do they think they're going to heaven if they blow themselves up like that?"

"Exactly. In fact, to some Muslims dying for jihad—holy war—is the only way to be sure they're going to make it to Paradise. Otherwise there's this big scale, and after a person dies all his good deeds are on one side, and the bad deeds are on the other."

"And the good has to outweigh the bad?"

"Yep."

"So how do Muslims know how they're doing?"

"They don't."

"No wonder they're so stressed."

"That's part of the reason so many of them are willing to blow themselves up."

"I'm glad I'm not a Muslim," Liz stated.

"Just being a woman is reason enough to be glad you're not, but that's a lesson for another day."

"OK," said Liz, although her curiosity had been aroused.

"Hey, wasn't this the day we were going to see the Sears Tower?" Sean reminded her.

"I'd love to."

"It's not the World Trade Center, but it is pretty impressive."

"Uh … Sean? Don't laugh at me, but …where's the World Trade Center?"

Sean sighed, shaking his head in a perfect Mike O'Brien impersonation.

"Lizzie, Lizzie, Lizzie…"

"Keep me as the apple of your eye;
hide me in the shadow of your wings
from the wicked who assail me,
from my mortal enemies who surround me."
—Psalm 17:8

Liz and Sean boarded the "L" and looked for a place to sit. There were plenty of choices. The only other passenger was a young man who seemed to be of Middle Eastern descent, who sat staring pensively out the window. Liz and Sean sat down across from him. The man glanced over at Liz, and when their eyes met, she smiled and said "hello." He quickly looked away and went back to staring out the window. Liz remembered what Sean had said about Muslims and women and wondered if Muslim men did not speak to women in public. She hoped she had not offended him, although she thought it odd that a smile and a greeting would be offensive. Maybe it was just this man.

At the next stop other people got on. A family of four boarded with cameras and maps that led Liz to believe they must be tourists. They didn't seem entirely used to riding a subway; Liz could relate. When her family had wanted to go to downtown St. Louis, they had just taken the Mercedes.

A tired-looking Hispanic woman in a blue-grey uniform stepped on and immediately took the seat right next to the door, heaving an exhausted sigh as she sat down. Liz wondered if she had been working all night. Her face was glistening with perspiration, and a wisp of hair persisted in dangling in her face; after a couple of attempts to brush it away, the lady gave up and sat with her head back and eyes closed as if catching a catnap before having to move again. The man who took the seat next to her was in direct contrast to the woman. He carried a laptop and wore a dark suit, white shirt, red tie, and a cell phone that seemed to be permanently attached to his ear, from which he was having a lively ongoing discussion. Oblivious to anyone or anything around him, he was absorbed in arranging meetings and collecting messages.

A young mother got on with a boy about five and a girl about two. The blonde, blue-eyed children resembled their attractive mother, although the mother had a haggard, worried look about her. The young boy kept asking her questions, mainly "Are we there yet?" and the mother tried to talk to them, but it was clear she was preoccupied with some grave concern. The little girl responded to Liz's smile by curling and uncurling her fingers—a two-year-old's version of a wave. Liz winked, and the little girl tried unsuccessfully to wink back.

"How soon are we going to see Daddy?" the boy asked his mother.

"Soon," said the mother absently, her voice breaking slightly. Her son didn't seem to notice.

"Are they going to let me an' Kaitlyn see him this time? Is he out of Expensive Care now?" The mother smiled sadly, pulled him closer to her, and whispered something in his ear.

Liz wondered about what this family was going through, and her imagination formed all kinds of dramatic scenarios until she decided that saying a silent prayer for them would be a much more productive use of her time.

But Liz found that her attention was repeatedly drawn back to the dark, mysterious stranger, the man who had not wanted to speak to her. He reminded her of the pictures in the book of Arabian Nights she and Elaine had loved to read when they were little girls. His eyes and skin were dark, his hair jet-black, his slender face chiseled and handsome, yet there was something about him that gave Liz a chill. One thing she began to notice was how nervous he seemed; his face had a sort of a wide-eyed look, and although he sat still as a statue for the most part, his fingers were fidgeting nonstop. Every few moments he glanced at his watch and stuck his hand in his pocket to feel something that was there.

An uneasy thought was forming in Liz's mind, a scenario she didn't want to consider. Snatches of her conversation with Mike over the breakfast table flashed through her mind and fed her imagination, which was already going into overdrive. Her heart began to pound, and she became short of breath. She looked over at Sean, but he was reading a newspaper he had bought that morning.

She began to have a detached feeling, as if she were watching the scene from outside. There seemed to be an evil presence filling the car—a darkness that was almost suffocating. Most of the other passengers didn't seem to be affected. The voices of the tourists and the businessman seemed far away, as if coming through a long tunnel. The toddler began to cry for no apparent reason. Was she feeling it, too, or was she just sensing her mother's stress? Liz closed her eyes as if to shut it all out.

Lord, help me. What's going on? she prayed.

She remembered a dream that had made her feel the same stark terror she was feeling now—a dream of being threatened and outnumbered, three to two. Only the two had been Jesus and her, and He had confronted her enemies and made them retreat with one word.

"The Lord is my Shepherd," [1] she recited silently. The Scripture gave her a glimmer of light. With her eyes closed she envisioned her Shepherd, staff in hand, standing between her and the ravenous wolves.

"Though I walk through the valley of the shadow of death…" [2]

More light.

Finally, her contemplation broke out into a direct prayer.

Help me, Jesus! What should I do? As the very thought of that Name came to her mind, she felt the panic begin to release its grip on her. She began to feel her Savior's presence, and a peace began to replace the fear. *Jesus…* Her heart slowed back down to normal, and she began to breathe normally. *Yes. Jesus.*

The L came to another stop. When Liz opened her eyes, the darkness seemed to have dissipated somewhat. She breathed deeply and made a conscious effort to relax.

I've been talking to Mike too much, she scolded herself.

The moment the doors were opened the businessman stepped out, still gripping his cell phone.

"See if you can get that meeting changed to later in the week, so I can contact…" His voice faded into the crowd as two more individuals boarded.

A young man in a tan uniform and a safari-type hat threw his large backpack down, startling the Middle Eastern man, and took the seat next to him. A plump, middle-aged woman in a brightly colored dress sat down on the other side with a certain deliberateness, as if the seat had her name on it. She said "Good mornin'!" in a musical voice with a Southern accent, but she received the same response as Liz had received earlier. The man stared ahead, obviously not wanting to engage himself in a conversation with her. She didn't seem to take the hint.

"Mah! It's hot, isn't it?" she panted. "Ah thought if Ah came up north it'd be a mite cooler, but not today! Whew! " She took out a handkerchief and began blotting the back of her neck. With thinly veiled irritation, Arabian Nights man folded his hands and closed his eyes as if praying or sleeping. The Southern lady spotted Liz, and Liz smiled.

"Are you from around here, darlin'?" she asked.

"I'm from St. Louis," Liz responded.

"Oh! With the awch?" she asked.

"Yes, that's the place," Liz answered. "Sean lives in the Chicago area, though." She turned to Sean, but he was still engrossed in his newspaper, or pretending to be. The Hispanic woman opened one eye momentarily to see the source of the annoying chatter.

"Ah flew over St. Louie once, and Ah saw that awch. Very impressive!"

"Where are you from?" Liz asked politely. There was something very familiar about this woman, but she couldn't think what it was.

"Alabama. Y'all been there?"

Liz shook her head.

"Oh, honey, you should visit there sometime. You'd think you'd dahd and gone to heaven!" She laughed a melodious laugh and continued to chatter away, as the man beside her continued to play possum so as not to get involved.

Meanwhile Liz's attention drifted from the talkative woman to the other passengers. As often happens when she was in a crowd, strangers she saw reminded her of people she knew. The man in the safari hat seemed very familiar, but then she had probably seen a uniform like that before. She thought the mailmen in St. Louis sometimes wore them, safari hat and all, but this man's backpack didn't seem like a mailbag at all.

Maybe he's a zookeeper, she thought. But if that were the case, what was in the backpack? Maybe medicine. *Maybe he's Dr. Livingston's great grandson, doing research in the Windy City,* she smiled. As she tried to think who he reminded her of, she noticed his hand moving ever so slowly toward the pocket of the dark stranger, who continued to "nap." The young man's eyes seemed to scan the group of people, each one preoccupied in one way or another. As he turned his head, his profile seemed all the more familiar to Liz. When his eyes met hers, she looked quickly back to the loquacious lady who continued her monologue.

"And the bougainvillea! Oh, honey, you should see it! It's gawgeous!"

Out of the corner of her eye Liz watched the pickpocket's hand continue to move unnoticed by anyone else. *He must not know I saw what he was doing,* she thought. She glanced over to Sean, who was still reading his paper, then to the woman telling her children that they were almost there, to the tired Hispanic lady, the family of tourists checking the batteries in their cameras, the chattering Scarlet O'Hara, and back to Lawrence of Arabia, who was oblivious to the fact that someone was lifting something out of his pocket.

Liz's heart began to pound again. She had never actually witnessed a crime happening. Her parents' house had been robbed once, but she had arrived after the fact, talking with the nice, safe policeman about what was missing. This was a whole different situation, and she was clueless as to what to do. She felt she ought to do something—but what? When dating the guy everyone in the theater department called "Country Boy," she had called herself "City Girl," since she had grown up in St. Louis. Now it occurred to her—what did she know? She was just a suburban girl—a *timid* suburban girl at that—with no idea where to turn for help on a subway full of strangers, and not about to make a citizen's arrest by herself. Was this man armed? He didn't seem like the type to have a gun, but then he didn't seem to be the type to pick people's pockets, either.

As if Liz's inexperience and timidity weren't enough, her emotions added to the confusion. The dark, cold man had frightened her at first, and even now she felt no particular duty to help him out. Safari Man had immediately seemed like an old friend to her, and while picking people's pockets certainly wasn't a good thing, still, she didn't feel threatened in the least by his presence. But then...

What's right is right, she told herself. She decided to do the right thing ... She decided to let Sean do the right thing.

"Sean?" she whispered. Sean didn't hear her. She nudged him. "Sean!" she said softly, not moving her lips. He looked up from the paper.

"Huh?"

Just then the car stopped and the doors opened again. The pickpocket stood up to leave. Liz hadn't realized how tall he was. Not that he was intimidating. Liz just felt that he was in control of the situation and that somehow everything was OK.

"Never mind," she said, looking away quickly.

"This is where we get off, kids," said the mother, and the little boy sang out, "Yaaaay!" He and his sister jumped up and down until their mother took them each firmly by the hand and guided them out.

"Goodness! That's mah stop already!" Southern Belle exclaimed. She got up and began to leave, then looked back, smiling. "It was nahce meeting you, Liz."

Being called by name by a total stranger took Liz by surprise. *Did I tell her my name?* she wondered. The woman was smiling knowingly.

"Uh, you too," Liz answered, but she was on automatic, her mind racing. As the lady stepped out, the young man in the tan uniform slipped the stolen item into his pocket, picked up his backpack, and stepped toward the door, just as the Middle Eastern man "woke up," checking out of the corner of his eye to see if the Southern chatterbox had left. As he slipped his hand automatically into his pocket, his face registered shock and dismay, then a sort of panic seized him; it appeared he too was at a loss as to what to do. Liz of course knew that the thief was heading toward the door, but again, when she tried to speak, she seemed paralyzed, incapable of doing or saying anything. It was as though an invisible hand had clamped tightly over her mouth.

At that moment she glanced over to see the young man pause in the doorway. (She could have *sworn* she knew him!) Looking directly at her, he winked and disappeared into the crowd.

"Home already?" asked Mike as Sean and Liz came into the den.

"Wha'd'you mean, 'already'?" said Sean. "We've been gone about three hours." Mike was seated at the computer, where Sean and Liz had left him that morning. "Have you been sitting there all day?"

"Hey, it's only noon. So how was the Sears Tower?"

"Awesome!" said Liz. "The view was amazing. The 'L' ride was pretty interesting, too. There was one passenger that scared me for a while. I probably have you to thank for that."

"Me?" Mike turned from the computer with a look of mild curiosity.

"Yeah… It was pretty silly. I saw a man that looked Middle Eastern that seemed to be acting sort of suspicious, and I started thinking about our conversation this morning. I almost freaked out.—Did you think he was acting suspicious, Sean?"

"That man you kept trying to talk to? I think he just didn't want to talk. People don't usually talk to people on the L."

"Hey, all I said was 'Hello'!" Liz stated defensively.

"And 'I'm from St. Louis' and 'Sean's from Chicago' and 'Where are you from?' I think his sitting there with his eyes closed should've told you something."

"I wasn't talking to him, I was talking to that Southern lady."

"What Southern lady?"

"The lady that was sitting next to the Middle Eastern guy." Sean said nothing, and his blank look surprised her. "I can't believe you didn't notice her, Sean. She was talking non-stop."

Sean looked puzzled and slightly amused. "The only one talking non-stop was you,

Liz. I saw a Hispanic lady. You mean her?" Liz's mouth dropped open in astonishment. Was Sean teasing her?

"No! The lady from Alabama."

"The one with the two kids?"

"No! The one that—" Liz was getting frustrated. "The lady right *across* from us, in the bright flowered dress! She was right next to the Middle Eastern man, and that guy in the safari hat was on the other side of him."

Sean laughed out loud. *"Safari hat!?"* Liz could feel her face getting hot. Mike seemed to be finding their conversation pretty entertaining. Liz thought of telling them how Jungle Jim had picked the other man's pocket and winked at her when he'd left, and how the Southern lady had called her "Liz" without Liz's having told her her name, but suddenly it all sounded so silly. All of a sudden she found herself short of breath.

"Liz, all I saw was an Arab guy sitting by himself on the subway with his eyes closed so he wouldn't have to talk to a red-headed chatterbox."

"A red-headed—?!" she gasped. She couldn't believe Sean was talking to her so flippantly. Sean immediately realized he had gone too far and began back-pedaling.

"A *lovely,* …*friendly,* … red-headed … stranger …" Sean was floundering, and Mike's smirk wasn't helping him any. Seeing Liz's eyes fill with tears, Sean tried to hug her, but she was so mortified she did the only thing she could think of doing; she fled to her room. The last thing she heard before slamming the door was Mike's voice saying, "nice goin', Bro."

OK, so now what? Liz thought. It had been an hour since she had barricaded herself in the guestroom to nurse her wounds. Her emotions were bouncing like a pinball from embarrassment to dread, to concern over what Sean's family was thinking of her, to anger with Sean for either not paying attention or not believing her, or both, to anger with herself for even bringing up the experience, to worrying over her own sanity.

She could hear Mrs. O'Brien downstairs in the kitchen, Pastor Dan coming in from the yard, and Shannon's stereo playing in her room, and her heart ached. They seemed like such a perfect family, and she really had started to feel like a part of it. Everything had been so perfect—*had* been. Now that a flaw in their relationship had reared its ugly head, it seemed to idealistic Liz that everything was utterly ruined. (Liz knew that this was an exaggeration, but her emotions were in too much of a binge of self-pity to let up now.) She allowed herself one more good cry, and when that had exhausted her, she indulged in ten minutes of staring out the window and sighing. Of course, this got boring in a hurry, and as the tide of emotion gradually subsided, she began to wonder if there was any way to save face and just pretend the whole stupid thing had never happened.

The knock on the door was well timed. Liz stole a quick glance in the mirror. Her eyes were still red, her hair only slightly disheveled. She ran a quick brush through it as she answered "Come in."

"Hey Liz!" came a chipper greeting as Shannon came in and jumped on the bed, bouncing Liz almost enough to snap her out of her pity party. "What'cha doin' up here?"

"Just …thinking ," Liz lied. When she thought about it, she hadn't been *thinking* at all, she'd been *emoting,* which is quite a different thing.

"You don't look too happy," Shannon observed. "Is Sean being a jerk?"

Liz sighed. "Not really."

"Mike being a jerk?"

"Not really," said Liz with half a smile.

"They're *both* being jerks!" Shannon guessed again. This produced the other half.

"I think there was just a misunderstanding," Liz admitted as the magnitude of the problem dissipated.

" 'Misunderstanding,' " Shannon nodded knowingly. "That's grownup code for '*everybody's* been a bit of a jerk, so let's forget the whole thing.' "

"Exactly!" Liz laughed out loud. "I think maybe I take myself too seriously," she confessed, then added with a twinge of annoyance, "I do wish other people would take me a little *more* seriously, though."

"I have a feeling this morning was one of those times?" Shannon guessed.

"Yeah. It was weird, Shannon. I witnessed a crime on the L today."

"A *crime?* Are you serious?!"

"Not only did Sean not see it, he didn't even remember seeing some of the people involved."

"Well, my brother's not always the most observant person in the world," Shannon chuckled.

"Well, what I saw was pretty odd, and when I started to describe it, I got laughed at, and that sorta ticked me off."

"Why did they laugh? What did you see?" Now Shannon was curious.

Liz was hesitant to get into it again, but something told her Shannon wouldn't laugh, or if she did, it wouldn't hurt as badly coming from her. She told Shannon exactly what she had seen.

When Liz was through, all Shannon said was, "So how come you didn't call the police?"

"I couldn't. I tried, but I couldn't say anything. And anyway, I didn't feel like it.—I know that sounds like a terrible excuse, but I mean, something told me it was OK. I had such peace when those two people got onto the car, and I'd been so freaked out by the Middle Eastern guy." She went on to tell Shannon about her thoughts of terrorism and desperately praying about it.

"Do you think my imagination got away from me?" she asked.

"I don't know, but I think I might have felt the same way," said Shannon. "You know, with Mike in the family, I hear a lot about that stuff. There's probably a lot more going on than most people know. I wonder if the two strange people were undercover cops."

"They were doing a pretty darn good job being undercover if nobody saw them except me."

"Yeah…" Shannon murmured thoughtfully. "Hmmm…"

There was a long pause.

"Shannon, what are you thinking?" Liz asked. She noticed that Shannon's reaction was nowhere close to Sean's, and it seemed almost as though her story had struck a familiar note. "Have you ever seen or heard something that nobody else did?"

Shannon hesitated for a moment.

"I haven't thought about it in years, but yeah, I think I have. When I was little, I got lost in a department store. I got scared, and I started to cry. Then a security guard, this sweet old man came along and asked me why I was crying. I remember his hair was white and wavy, and he had the bluest eyes I've ever seen," she added, smiling wistfully.

"When I told him I couldn't find my mom, he said he knew where she was. (It didn't occur to me to wonder how he knew *who* my mother was, much less *where* she was.) He took out a big, clean white handkerchief, dried my tears, and took me by the hand. He walked me right to where Mom was searching frantically for me. She was so relieved to see me, she scooped me up and hugged and kissed me, but she didn't say anything to the security guy. Later when she was telling Dad about it at dinner, I told him about the nice old man with the blue eyes who had taken me to her, and she didn't remember having seen him at all. Then she and Dad got into a discussion of little kids and their imaginations. It kinda made me mad, even at that age."

"Well, it's *infuriating* when you're twenty-three!" Liz complained.

"Well, I know I saw that man, and by the way, I believe you about this morning."

"Thanks, Shannon," said Liz. She had never expected to be so encouraged by someone so much younger, but she appreciated Shannon's being there, and her being transparent with her. Having someone believe her also helped alleviate her feelings that she was losing her mind.

At that moment they could hear Mrs. O'Brien's voice, calling everyone to lunch. Liz groaned, feeling mortified all over again.

"What do I do, Shannon?" she asked.

"Nothing. Just go down and act like nothing's happened."

"You don't think Sean and Mike will mention it?"

"Not if they have half a brain between them," Shannon snickered. "But if they do, don't get mad, just laugh it off and don't take yourself so seriously, ya little perfectionist!"

"Boy, can you read people!"

"Yeah, it's a gift. Just remember, nobody's perfect."

Liz smiled. "Not even us?"

"Nope. And *especially* not them!" Shannon laughed, cocking her head toward the young men bounding down the stairs to the dining room.

CHAPTER SEVENTEEN

Liz was glad that age differences didn't matter to Shannon in the least. She was happy to show Liz the mall while Sean was training; in fact, she seemed to enjoy being the tour guide. Soon the two of them were acting like typical American girls, sharing opinions about products and guys and "Do these earrings make my butt look big?" They laughed together at the funny greeting cards and sampled fragrances until their "smellers" were too confused to tell the difference, then talked about life over a cappuccino.

"Life with Jesus … is like a cappuccino," Shannon mused.

Suppressing a smirk, Liz replied, "Do tell!"

Shannon's philosophical air wasn't all that convincing, but she laid it on thick as she stared into her cup. "First, it exudes the 'aroma of Christ' … or it's supposed to, anyway." She breathed in the steam and took a lick of whipped cream. "It's sweet and light at first, which is nice, but then when you get past the fluff …" She slurped loudly. "…you get something more substantial and energizing!"

"And … it's brown," Liz observed, keeping a serious face to see what Shannon would say next.

"Yes, it's brown. That's deep, Liz." Her lips tightened, but the laughter escaped through her nose. Liz chuckled.

"Aren't we the philosophers?"

"Yeah … I don't think Pastor Dillingham has anything to worry ab—Oh, *brother! Give me a **break**!*" She sounded so disgusted that Liz turned around to see the source of such outrage.

A worker in the lingerie shop on the corner was hanging a giant poster in the window, showing several buxom beauties posing in next-to-nothing—the next-tonothings coming in various colors. Although displays like this were nothing new, the novelty of this one was the white feathered wings on each model. The slogan said something about angels.

"Man! People are so clueless!" Shannon grumbled. "'Angels,' my … cappuccino!"

"Yeah, I guess the real ones aren't exactly like that," Liz agreed.

"Y'know, I was reading in the Old Testament the other day…" (Liz loved the way Shannon grew suddenly animated when sharing something she had discovered in the Bible.) "…where the armies of Israel were hugely outnumbered by their enemies—There was this army of 185,000 coming against them! God sent one angel, and that angel wiped out the whole army in a single blow!"

"Wiped out the 185,000?!"

"Yep. One angel did that." With a scornful glance at the poster, Shannon added, "and I bet that angel wasn't some chick in satin underwear. Mall theology!" she snorted.

"Yeah. Lingerie and cappuccinos."

"I guess we'd better get back soon," said Shannon. "Sean's probably done with the training session, and he'd be mad at me if I hogged you all evening, too," she added with a mischievous look in her eye that hinted she was thinking of doing it anyway.

"I'm ready any time you are," said Liz.

"OK, but first I want to say 'hi' to a friend."

They disposed of their coffee cups, and Liz followed Shannon, who turned and entered the jewelry store around the corner.

"Hey, Missy!" she greeted the young girl behind the counter.

"Shannon! Hi! W'sup?"

"Just hangin' out with—Oh, I'm sorry—Melissa, this is Liz, Sean's girlfriend. She's visiting from St. Louis."

"Oh wow, the place with the golden arches?"

"That's McDonald's, Miss'."

"Just kidding. Hi!"

"Hi, Missy," said Liz. "Wow, what a nice place to work." She was dazzled by the sparkling merchandise.

"Yeah, it's a tough job, but somebody's got to do it," she quipped. "Daddy won't let me take home samples, though," she added with a pout.

"Anything new?" Shannon asked, admiring the glittering pendants and matching earrings.

"Nothing in your price range, girl!"

"Hey, who said anything about price? Looking's free, right, Liz?"

Liz just smiled.

"I may as well show you the good stuff, then," Missy said, making her way to a display case full of diamond rings. "Check these out," she said, pointing to an elegant set of engagement/wedding rings. "They just came in yesterday. Look at that classic design. I just love that kind of ring!"

"Yeah, engagement rings," Shannon laughed. "Anybody particular in mind? Maybe whose initials are KP?" Missy blushed and gave Shannon a friendly punch. Then she turned to Liz, who was gazing at a ring with a design unlike anything she had ever seen before.

"Do you like that one?" Missy asked.

"It's beautiful!" Liz sighed. "So unique."

Missy reached into the case and got the ring out. "Here, try it on. Trying on's free, too," she grinned.

"Oh, that's OK," Liz protested weakly. "I don't need to…"

"Go ahead, Liz," said Shannon. "You're closer to that sort of thing than Missy is," she added, dodging the next swipe from her friend.

Liz slipped the ring on and marveled at the graceful way the band came together around the cluster of diamonds. "It's gorgeous," she murmured, staring at it for a moment. "I've never seen anything like it." Still in a philosophical mood, she began to see it as a picture of a Christian family—a couple of diamonds set intimately together, several tiny diamonds, like children gathered around them, and the whole setting surrounded by the golden arms of God, holding them together. Her mind began to wander, but she caught herself. *Don't go there,* a little voice inside warned, and she quickly removed the ring and handing it back to Missy. "Thanks," she said, hoping her face wasn't as red as it felt.

She began browsing again, mainly as an excuse to turn away from the other girls, so she didn't see Shannon grinning at her friend. Missy looked at Liz and back at Shannon with a questioning look, and Shannon gave her a silent thumbs-up.

"Hi Mom!" called Shannon as she and Liz came in through the kitchen door. Mrs. O'Brien was coming up from the basement with a basket of laundry to fold, but the aroma of a pot roast told the girls she had been busy in the kitchen as well.

"Hi girls. How was the mall?"

"Fun. Where's dinner?" Shannon asked, rummaging through the cupboards.

"Now don't be gettin' a snack, dear," said Mrs. O'Brien, her Irish dialect kicking in as she was giving the orders. "Dinner's in half an hour."

"But we're *starved!*" Shannon whined. Liz decided not to enter this conversation, lest she get cornered into confessing about the cappuccino, the cinnamon-roasted almonds, and the giant pretzels. (Hey, a girl's gotta eat.)

"Hang in there, ye'll survive," Mrs. O'Brien reassured her, carrying the basket upstairs. Shannon waited until she was out of sight then proceeded to pull out a box of cereal.

"Want some?" she offered Liz.

"I'd better not. I've had so much already today. Calorie overload," she explained, patting her stomach.

"Oh, you mean the stuff we had at the mall? First of all, we ate the pretzels while walking through the mall, so those calories don't count."

"Really?" Liz asked, amused.

"Yeah, if you eat while walking, the calories get canceled out."

"We were sitting when we had the mocha cappuccinos, though."

"But they were buy-one-get-one-free, so the second one doesn't count. Besides, coffee doesn't have any calories."

"But chocolate, sugar, and whipped cream do."

"Oh well, those calories were probably hiding in that second drink, which doesn't count anyway, because we didn't pay for it."

Liz snickered. "I like your reasoning. Tell me more."

"OK," said Shannon. "These calories," she said, tapping the cereal box, "don't count, because it's a breakfast cereal, and breakfast time expired *hours* ago."

"So if you share any with me, that doesn't count, either." Liz was catching on.

"Oh, sharing means minus calories." Shannon took a handful of cereal, crammed it into her mouth, and opened the refrigerator door. To Liz's surprise, she leaned in, took a swig from the milk bottle, mixed it with the cereal in her mouth, and swallowed it with a satisfied grin.

"See?" she explained. "The milk bottle never came out of the fridge, so those calories don't count, either."

"Do you always do that?" asked Liz, feeling a little queasy.

"No, I just feel a little crazy today. Maybe you've been a bad influence on me," she added with her most nauseatingly "innocent" look.

"Me?!" exclaimed Liz with her most indignant drop of the jaw, trying hard to keep a straight face. "When did I ever drink your family's milk right out of the bottle?"

"Oh, I'm sorry," said Shannon sincerely, holding the bottle out to her. "Did you want some?" Liz shook her head emphatically.

"Not now, I don't."

"Oooo!" Shannon had spotted something else. She reached into the refrigerator and pulled out a can of whipped cream. "RediWhip!" She snapped the cap off and began squirting it into her mouth just as Sean stepped into the room.

"Hey, little sis!" he scolded. "Where are your manners? What have I taught you about RediWhip?" Shannon froze, her mouth full.

"Sthare?" was the muffled guess as she offered him the can.

"Darn right," he said, grabbing the can and squirting a mound into his own mouth. He then politely held it out to Liz, who was laughing so hard she couldn't speak.

"I hear footsteps!" cried Shannon in a hoarse whisper.

"Mom!" Sean guessed, quickly capping the RediWhip and slipping it out of sight. Shannon shoved the box of cereal back into the pantry, and they both stood there with their most nonchalant expressions, while Liz tried to stifle a laugh that was threatening to come out her nose. This wasn't easy, since Sean had a dab of whipped cream on the end of his chin, which he was apparently unaware of.

But the person coming into the kitchen was not Mrs. O'Brien but Mike, and he made no comment about Sean's fashion accessory but got right to the point.

"Sean, Liz, come here, you've got to see something." He looked and sounded so serious that they all followed him immediately to the den.

The computer screen displayed a news article featuring a photo of a very familiar face. Liz started as she recognized the Middle Eastern man she had seen on the subway.

"Look familiar?" asked Mike, seeing the look on Liz's face.

Liz had a hard time catching her breath. "Uh…yeah…" she replied absently, reading the headlines, which said,

"Terror Suspect Arrested in Chicago"

"What's going on?" Sean wanted to know, trying to read over Liz's shoulder.

"He was arrested late this morning," Mike explained, "about the time you guys were out on your way to the Sears Tower. Someone at the subway station thought he was acting suspicious. They found all kinds of explosives on him. They think he was going to try to blow up the Sears Tower." Mike was talking to Sean, but he watched Liz's reactions out of the corner of his eye.

"You're kidding…" Sean murmured, reading the details.

Mike continued while Liz stared, speechless. "He was detained while the bomb squad was checking out all the paraphernalia he had strapped to himself. They defused it all, but one thing that was kind of weird…there was no detonator. No one knows how he had planned to set the stuff off."

"That is strange," Sean commented. Now he was watching Liz, too, waiting for her to say something. "Liz, this guy does look familiar. Is he the one you thought was acting suspicious on the L?"

"*Very* suspicious," she recalled, and she noticed Shannon was looking into her eyes, wordlessly urging her to say more. "And I think I know what happened to the detonator," she added. *I can't believe I'm bringing this up again!* she thought. Sean and Mike were silently listening, and neither one looked as if he were going to laugh this time. "Someone stole it, took it right out of his pocket. I saw it happen." There was dead silence as this revelation sank in.

"Who … ?" Sean began.

Liz sighed, braced herself for more humiliation, and said, "This man … in a safari hat." No one was laughing, so she added, "while the Middle Eastern man had his eyes closed to shut out the Southern lady and her chatter."

There was a long pause, after which Shannon broke the silence.

"Angels," she whispered. "That's what *I* think they were."

"Or undercover agents?" Mike wondered out loud.

"Yeah, Bro," Shannon scoffed. "Undercover agents invisible to Sean."

"Maybe we'll get more details on tonight's news," Liz suggested.

"I doubt it," said Mike. "This kind of stuff isn't usually publicized much. Bad for tourism."

Sean looked stunned. He stared at the computer screen again, trying to piece everything together. "That *was* the guy on the L," he said softly. "I could have *sworn* he was sitting alone…"

Mike sat back in the swivel chair, looking pensive.

"I don't think any of us is ever as alone as we think," he mused.

That day, after Liz had explained in detail everything she had remembered about the ride on the L, Sean repented in sackcloth and ashes….well, not really, but he did give Liz a solemn promise that he would never again take her experiences lightly, even when—*especially* when—he didn't understand them.

"We have different gifts," he reasoned. "And yours seems to be seeing things that others don't. I'm so glad you followed your gut instinct and prayed!"

"It wasn't much of a prayer," said Liz sheepishly.

"Well, you quoted God's Word, and you called on the name of Jesus. Apparently that was enough to bring us a couple of angels."

"I think we probably should do that more," Liz admitted. "We take so much for granted, like safety—and life!"

I guess Mike would say that's because we're *'complacent, spoiled Americans,'"* said Sean, imitating Mike perfectly.

From that day on, Liz and Sean prayed together each morning. They asked the Lord for His protection for themselves and for each of their families, although with their wearing a path from Chicago to St. Louis, they were beginning to seem like two branches of the same family, different as they were.

Sean had spent time with Liz's parents one evening when she and Elaine had been having some "girl time." Liz even saw Sean and Elaine having a private conversation that came to an abrupt halt when she entered the room. And of course, Sean couldn't wait to meet the cousins.

As for Sean's family, Liz had shopped with Shannon, baked with Colleen, and been enlightened by Mike. The only one she had not spent any one-on-one time with was Sean's father, "Pastor Dan." But that was about to change.

In fact, her whole life was about to change.

CHAPTER EIGHTEEN

Tonight was the night "Pastor Dan" was taking Liz to dinner at a nice restaurant, where they would have several hours to get to know one another better. Liz was past the stage where she felt she was being evaluated; she knew she had passed the test long ago. But this morning when Liz came downstairs, Shannon and her mother abruptly stopped their conversation upon seeing her; the first and last word she had heard was "tonight." This date, she suspected, might have another purpose, such as getting her out of the house. What was Sean planning?

She knew Sean was a planner, and that he had a knack for making everyday things special. When she had first come to visit his family, it wasn't enough for him merely to make sure the guest room was tidy and the bathroom stocked with towels. He had brought fresh flowers in from the garden to adorn the room, and had even left chocolate kisses on the pillow with a note that said, "Sweet dreams." In the bathroom there was scented oil by the tub, and on the dressing table, reflected in the mirror, was a single red rose, complete with a fern and baby's breath, in a Coke bottle. The sight of it had brought back warm memories of his first anonymous expression of affection for her when they were in the theater department at school. During the stressful spring musical, it had been a happy distraction for her to see it reflected in the dressing-room mirror.

Now it seemed that Sean was once again "up to something," and that everyone in the family knew about it except her. There were meaningful glances exchanged, sly smiles, and someone's asking Dan how far away the restaurant was and how fast the service was there. Obviously, timing was a consideration.

Consequently, Liz was nervous about that night. It wasn't the time spent with

Pastor Dan, since he had a way of putting her at ease, but more the question of what awaited her when they got home. What sort of unique drama did Sean have prepared? And was he going to ask her what she thought (and hoped) he might ask her? And if he did, what would she say? *Stupid question,* she thought. She had known for months that Sean was the one for her. There had been no angel appearing in the sky to tell her "This is it!" But there was that peace she had when she was with him, especially when they prayed together, and the way she felt somehow incomplete when they were apart.

She sometimes thought the "proper Christian thing to do" would be to isolate herself from the world, maybe fast for forty days and ask the Lord if Sean was the one. She had known people who had done that, and felt somewhat guilty for not wanting to herself. She could picture herself, on the brink of starvation, pleading with God for an answer, and having the Lord say, as Shannon would, "Well, *DUH…!*"

No, she had prayed *for* Sean and *about* Sean and *with* Sean, and it was really pretty obvious, not only to them but to anyone who knew them. She didn't have to pray for an answer; Sean *was* the answer. The question wasn't the "M" word, it was whether or not tonight they'd become … the "E" word.

Liz found herself debating what to wear, even though she had brought only two outfits. The purple dress was a bit flashy, and she didn't know if it would be appropriate if this turned out to be a "solemn occasion." The black suit was pretty business-like and somehow not quite festive enough. She finally settled on wearing the purple dress with the black blazer. After checking herself in the mirror several times too many, she finally had to remind herself that Sean's family loved *her,* not her clothes, and besides, if tonight turned out to be nothing monumental, she would feel pretty foolish for obsessing so. However, as she came downstairs, the whole family was there, as if they were sending her and Dan off on a European vacation.

"You look nice," Sean commented. It was an innocent enough remark, but somehow he reminded Liz of a small child with chocolate on his face and a stolen, half-eaten brownie behind his back. The others just smiled as though posing for a family portrait. *OK, something's going on,* Liz thought, and she got that same flutter of excitement she used to get before a performance.

"Well, shall we go?" said Pastor Dan as he opened the door. "We'll see you later," he added to the others, who seemed to be standing around with nothing in particular to do. Or waiting until they left before springing into action.

It was hard for Liz to focus on dinner that night—not that she was holding her menu upside down or anything, but her mind was more on what was going on back at the house. At first she was fumbling for something to say and wondering how they could fill the entire meal with conversation when they were both obviously preoccupied.

It then occurred to her that there was still a great deal she didn't know about Sean's family. Could she ask Pastor Dan some of the questions that had come to mind in recent days without coming across as prying or conducting an interview? She decided it would be better than staring at the centerpiece all evening and watching the awkwardness escalate. So, after the waiter took their order, she asked, "So, when exactly did you and your wife meet?"

"Oh…" Pastor Dan hesitated, his brow creased as he concentrated. "I believe it was 1970. Colleen's better with dates than I am. I was on a mission trip to Ireland with my church group that summer."

"That's interesting. You don't hear much about missions to Ireland. Aren't there already a lot of churches there? I mean, I thought the Irish were Catholic."

"The ones that aren't Protestant, yes. Roll?"

"Thank you."

"How many actual Christians there are is hard to tell. The mission was evangelistic, but the approach was peace-making."

"'Blessed are the peace-makers,'" Liz quoted. Pastor Dan smiled.

"Easier said than done," he sighed as the smile faded. "Emotions were pretty intense over there. Colleen's brother was especially passionate about his 'cause' and one night was in the wrong place at the wrong time." He paused as the words sank in.

"He was—?" Liz began and hesitated to finish the thought.

"Killed," Pastor Dan confirmed.

"How *awful!*"

"Colleen's parents were devastated, of course, and Colleen … well, she was like a lost lamb when I met her. When we shared the gospel with her, she was like someone in the desert drinking water for the first time in … well, you get the idea. The transformation was immediate. The peace Christ gave her … we could see it in her eyes. It was wonderful." Pastor Dan's own eyes were shining with the memory. "After I came home, we wrote to each other. I tried to encourage her in her new faith, but I think she ran circles around me. I was so taken with her childlike attitude toward God, and yet I was impressed with her maturity. But then there was a lot of political upheaval going on where she was, so I guess her faith had to grow or die."

"I never thought much about it, but I guess it's easy to stagnate when life is too easy," said Liz.

"Then thank God for trials," the pastor concluded. "Up until then I had never thought that someone could fall in love with another person thousands of miles away, but I grew fonder of her the more we wrote."

"So when did you see her again?"

"A year later I went back to Ireland—"

"Another mission trip?"

"Yep. The church was impressed with my zeal," he added with a wink. "I met up with Colleen, and one look told me that I had indeed fallen in love with her. And one look from her told me she felt the same. I know it sounds crazy, but I proposed to her within a week."

"And she said 'yes'!"

"She did."

"I love happy endings … or I guess in this case it was a happy beginning."

"Not quite. Her parents weren't happy at all. They were still grieving over their son, and the fact that I was a Protestant sort of made me the enemy."

"But you were there as a peace-maker!" Liz protested.

"I guess they weren't interested in peace. To them it was as though I had killed Sean myself."

"Sean?"

"Yes, Colleen's brother's name was Sean. Anyway, they felt betrayed and wanted nothing to do with our marriage."

"That's so *sad!* So that explains why Colleen never says anything about her family in Ireland."

"No, she'd rather focus on the family she has now."

"And a wonderful family it is," said Liz. It came out sounding cornier than she had intended, but she meant every word.

Between the salad and the main course the conversation turned to Michael.

"I didn't realize Michel was such a little terror!" Liz exclaimed after a few "young Mikey" stories. "Thank you," she said as the waiter set down her entrée.

"Well, being a PK is OK for some kids, (Thank you.) but it can bring out the worst in others. Mikey resented the expectations put on him from day one. We tried to let him be a normal kid, but there were always members of the congregation that expected more. Usually well-meaning elderly ladies who used phrases like 'Now wouldn't you think the preacher's son would…'" (Liz giggled at the pastor's squeaky imitation of their voices.) " … followed by some uprighteous expression of 'disappointment.'"

"Uprighteous?"

"One of Mikey's words. He had learned a few … shall we say 'choice phrases?' as a child and used them at the most inopportune times. Later he got more creative and started making up words of his own, like 'uprighteous' and 'hypocriticism.'"

"Those words actually kinda make sense."

"Absolutely! Mike was never dumb. However, he could be pretty unwise sometimes. In his teens he sure gave his mother and me a lot of grey hairs and sleepless nights. Finally his antics went too far, and landed him in Juvie."

"Juvenile detention?"

"Bingo."

"Really …" Liz had a hard time picturing Sean's ultra-conservative brother in a jail cell.

"Yep. Hit rock bottom, praise God."

"Praise God?"

"Best thing that could've happened to him. He had everything taken away from him so he could share a room with a very sick drunk. Between the noise and the stench, he realized he wasn't exactly living the Abundant Life."

"So he finally started listening to you?"

Pastor Dan sighed. "Not me. Another pastor. A youth worker. He had a regular ministry at Juvie and connected with Mike. I guess he had a similar story (receiving a lot of hypocriticism from the uprighteous) and understood how Mike ended up where he was. He kind of took Mike under his wing and discipled him, something Mike would never let me do."

"Wow, that's kind of ironic," said Liz.

"It was a growing experience for me, too," said Pastor Dan, pensively taking a sip of his water. "I had to learn to let go of my ego and just be glad someone had reached my son, even if it wasn't me."

"That *would* be a challenge," said Liz. "I never thought of pastors' getting jealous, but I guess it happens to everybody."

"The *really* ironic thing," said Pastor Dan, "was that after Mike had repented of everything he had done, he became more strong-willed than ever. Only this time his attention went beyond his little self-centered world. Shocking the little old ladies at church wasn't going to satisfy him any more. He wanted his impact on the world to reach farther and accomplish something more significant."

"So how did he get so … current-event-savvy?"

"He was involved in a large gathering of Christians in Washington, D.C., and when he came home and read about it in the paper, he realized their account bore little resemblance to what he had observed with his own eyes. He wrote his first letter to the editor, telling 'the truth' from his point of view. He worked so hard on that letter. Then he found out that editors edit."

"Excuse me?"

"The letter he had written so meticulously had been cut down 'for space' and didn't have the original wallop. He was livid. He began checking out alternative news sources and becoming more aware of world events and their ramifications. His passion was channeled toward spreading the 'Truth,' especially when it collided with mainstream media's versions that the public swallowed hook, line, and sinker on a regular basis."

"So he decided to major in journalism?"

"With the help of a social studies teacher at his high school. He recognized Mike's zeal and flair for writing. He also noticed Mike liked to argue—he and that teacher hardly ever agreed on anything! But the teacher was mature enough to appreciate that at least the kid was thinking. He said some very complimentary things about Mike when we met him. He's the one who suggested Mike go into journalism."

"Well, it seems natural, the way he likes to debate."

"He'd probably make a good lawyer, too," Pastor Dan laughed. "But he'd probably have to wear a tie.—How's your salmon?"

"Delicious. I think I'm going to need a box, though … Actually, when you talk to Mike about politics, he seems like the type that would wear a tie. How come …?"

"How come he dresses like a kid? I think it's to relate to the people around him. Sometimes a suit and tie can alienate certain people, the very ones he wants to communicate 'Truth' to."

"So it's an evangelism strategy?"

"Well, that and he likes to be comfortable." Pastor Dan chuckled. "And the baggy pants drive his mother crazy. That's a plus as far as he's concerned. Some things never change."

By the time they had finished the main course, the conversation had dwindled, and Liz seemed to be "on automatic." Occasionally she would realize with some discomfort that she was not one hundred per cent sure what she had just said. If Pastor Dan noticed, he didn't show it. Liz saw him glance at his watch more than once, and when she declined his offer of dessert, he seemed disappointed and glanced at his watch again. He lingered over his coffee, even though the check sat by his cup. Finally he got out his credit card and handed it to the waiter.

"I'm not a big fan of credit," he told Liz, as if having to explain himself. "I don't believe in buying things you can't pay for. It is a convenience, though."

"Yes, it is," agreed Liz, who was only half listening. After a brief, awkward pause, the waiter came back. Dan signed the check and put the card back in his wallet.

"I've always taught my kids that a credit card is a tool, not a license," he said. "They're to be paid in full every month, and if you ever find you can't pay it in full and on time, it's time to cut up the card." He sounded as though he had made this speech more than once before, and Liz thought he was probably on automatic, too.

"That's a good rule to go by," she said when she sensed it was her turn to say something. How soon could they go on to the *real* reason for the evening?

When finally they were heading back to the car, Dan asked Liz, "Hey, you wanna go by the new church building on the way home?" (*Still stalling,* she thought.)

"Sure, OK."

"You've never seen the inside, have you?"

"No, I haven't, but I'd love to."

"Great. I think I've got a key," he said, fingering his collection of keys. "Yep, here it is," he added with satisfaction.

They drove for about ten minutes until they turned off onto an unpaved road. Dan slowed down as the car was jostled by the unevenness. The grounds were not landscaped yet, and the parking lot was unpaved, but the church itself looked very much completed. Liz had to step carefully to avoid small puddles as she got out of the car and headed for the entrance. Pastor Dan unlocked the building and stepped inside.

"Hang on, I'll get the lights." He found the switch and turned on the lights in the foyer. Liz stepped through the door and was greeted with the combined smell of sawdust, drywall, and paint. Their footsteps echoed off the walls as they made their way toward the large double doors leading into the sanctuary. Liz found herself intrigued in spite of her earlier preoccupation.

"Are you ready?" Pastor Dan asked, drumming his fingers on the door to add suspense.

"Yes!" Liz cried, and he opened the doors with a flourish.

Other than needing a little more paint and carpeting, the church was impressively close to completion. The pews were installed, and at the front an altar was already in place. And even as the pastor was reaching for the light switch, Liz noticed another source of light already in the room; at the far end of the sanctuary, there were two candles lit on the altar. And between them, standing in front of the altar was someone familiar.

"Hi, Liz," said Sean. His voice carried well in the uncarpeted sanctuary. She had a flashback of another moment in a sanctuary where she had sat alone (or so she had thought) praying fervently for direction in her life. Sean had shown up then, too, and the simple words "Hi, Liz," had been the beginning of a major turning point in her life. Now here he was again.

"Hi, Sean," she said shyly. Suddenly she was aware that Pastor Dan had disappeared.

"I've got something to ask you," Sean said, his voice a little shaky.

"OK," she answered, her own voice barely audible. As he stood there, it dawned on her that he didn't want to shout the question across the sanctuary, so she slowly made her way down the center aisle. When she got to where Sean was standing, he took her hand as she walked up the steps onto the platform.

"Do you think you could do this again sometime?" he asked.

"Do what?" she asked, almost afraid to assume he meant what she was thinking.

"Come down the aisle… to me." Liz stared at him. In spite of her earlier suspicions and long thought-out answers, she now found herself speechless.

"Marry me, Liz." Her eyes shone, and a smile crept across her lips.

"OK," she said, grinning. *So much for a fine acceptance speech…*

Sean embraced her impulsively, laughing for joy.

"I hear music, Sean."

"Yeah, I'm happy, too!" he laughed.

"No, really. I hear *music!*" she insisted. Sean laughed again. He turned to the back of the church.

"She said 'Yes!'" he announced to the balcony. Dan, Colleen, Mike, and Shannon (who had been playing the guitar and softly singing) all cheered. Liz gasped, then laughed, then let Sean take both her hands in his, as his family had the habit of doing. He looked down at them and frowned.

"Liz," he scolded. "You let it get tarnished again."

"Oops."

"Give it here." Liz handed him the silver ring, thinking he must be awfully flustered; polishing her ring was sometimes what he did when he didn't know what to say. Sean pulled a wadded up rag from his pocket and began polishing as he had so many times before.

"Here," he said tenderly, taking her hand and slipping the ring onto her finger. "You're all set."

Liz looked down at her hand and gasped again. This wasn't her silver ring; that one was now in Sean's pocket. This one, glistening in the candlelight, had a cluster of diamonds with the gold band wrapped around them like the arms of God. It was the one from the jewelry store she had fallen in love with.

"Did Shannon…?"

"Of course," said Sean smugly.

"Blabbermouth!" she said loudly toward the balcony. Shannon giggled.

"Hey, you know what they say. 'The family that proposes together…'"

"I don't think that's quite how it goes, but this was quite a group effort," Liz marveled. "So your whole family was involved?"

"Plus Shannon's friend Missy. She also drove us here so there wouldn't be a car in the parking lot."

"The music was Sean's idea!" Shannon announced. "I told him it was too corny, but he wouldn't listen."

"Oh my gosh. I knew something was going on, but I had no idea it was going to happen here."

"Well, I wanted our engagement to begin and end the same way, with you walking down the aisle."

"Mr. Drama," she sighed.

"And I want it to begin and end with one more thing," he added. Liz knew what he meant even before he turned toward the altar; she turned and knelt with him.

As the rest of the family quietly slipped out, Sean and Liz, hand in hand, bowed their heads and asked the Lord to bless their relationship, their marriage, and their family.

What they didn't know was that God was about to show them miracles sooner than they thought—long before they would become husband and wife.

CHAPTER NINETEEN

Before they knew it, Liz and Sean were back in St. Louis. They had wanted to break the news to Liz's parents in person, although it was all Liz could do to contain herself on the phone. She managed to keep the conversations short, only requesting that her mother get "Sean's room" ready and hinting that "We've got lots of news, but we'll tell you when we get there."

Even when they first arrived, it was all small talk until that Saturday. Liz and Sean had been watching for an opportune time to approach both Rachel and George together. Finally that evening they found the two of them relaxing in the den.

"Mr. Danfield?" Sean began, and Liz noted a quiver in his voice.

"Please, call me 'George!'" Liz's dad insisted.

"Uh, George …"

Liz held her breath. This was the moment they had rehearsed. Sean was going to "do it right" and ask George for his daughter's hand in marriage. Of course, they would never have agreed to take this approach of they'd had any doubt what George's answer would be.

"Yes?" George responded, peering over his reading glasses.

Sean's serious expression turned into a wide grin. "She said 'yes.'"

What? thought Liz. This wasn't what they had prepared. But she saw her father's face break into a big smile and her mother's eyes fill with tears.

"Please! Call me 'Dad!'" George now insisted. He set down the paper, stuffed his glasses in his pocket, and abruptly left the room. Liz had a fleeting mental picture of him returning with a shotgun or a baseball bat, something he had often kidded about when she was a teenager, but she knew deep down that her father liked Sean, and her fiancé was in no danger.

She was still pondering Sean's abandonment of the script when George came back with four glasses and a bottle of champagne that was already chilled.

"A toast!" George announced, pouring each person a glass. "To the happy couple!" This was not the sort of celebrating Liz and Sean usually did, but they took the glasses without hesitation.

"And to wonderful in-laws!" Sean added as the glasses clinked. Rachel, still teary-eyed, hugged Sean with her free arm.

"Welcome to the family!" she cried.

"Wait a minute," said Liz. "Why do I get the feeling you guys aren't all that surprised?" Her parents exchanged glances with Sean. "Sean was supposed to ask you for permission to marry me."

"Oh honey, he did," said Rachel.

"He did? When?"

"Last time you were here," George explained. When you and Elaine were getting the Chinese carry-out that night, he and I had a little man-to-man."

"He did a very nice job, too," Rachel added. "In spite of your father's trying to intimidate him."

"Hey, it was a once-in-a-lifetime opportunity. I wanted to enjoy it."

"Elizabeth, he sat there acting as though he were sizing Sean up and trying to decide if he was good enough or if he should just throw him out—poor dear!"

"It would have worked too, if you hadn't started gushing and going on and on about 'you're such a fine young man' and how wonderful it all was," George tried to look mad at his wife for blowing his cover, but by the way he was chuckling, Liz could tell this was a story he would tell often.

"So you asked them before you asked me!" Liz exclaimed, realizing that of the four she was the only one surprised that night.

"Hey, you said we should do it right," Sean pointed out.

"So I did."

CHAPTER TWENTY

"Sing in the choir?" asked Liz. Since she had found her own apartment and joined the church early in September, she had thought she was participating in just about every activity the church had to offer; she even had a part-time job helping in the office. "I haven't sung in a choir since high school."

"So it's high time you did it again," Sean reasoned. Liz hadn't seen him this excited since she had accepted his marriage proposal. "They're doing Handel's *Messiah* this Christmas! The whole thing—with a full orchestra! The new sanctuary will be ready by then, and they're going to make Christmas Eve the first service there. It's going to be *awesome!* And," he added with a tone of profound veneration, "You'll get to experience *Charles Walker.*"

Oh yeah, Liz thought, *Mr. Walker.* She had met him when she had first come to Faith Chapel and had seen him direct the choir almost every Sunday since. Sean's parents had related the story of the Christmas Eve when ten-year-old Sean had announced, "When I grow up, I want to be Mr. Walker." As a child, Sean had sometimes been seen in his bedroom playing music on his tape player and conducting an invisible company of singers and musicians. Although Sean's aspirations had changed somewhat, Charles Walker was still, and probably always would be, a role model for him. Almost every adult in the church called him "Chuck," but Sean, who was not yet feeling quite like an adult, and never feeling anything close to the man's equal, continued to call him "Mr. Walker," with the utmost reverence. Liz, being relatively new to the church, did the same.

Charles Walker was not a large man, or in any way one that could easily be spotted in a crowd. His gray hair was thinning, and glasses obscured the brightness of his eyes.

His dress and his movements were about what one would expect of a man in his early sixties. Someone Sean and Liz's age might easily pass him by without a second glance.

But when he spoke, one was suddenly struck by the passion in his voice—a passion for his music, a passion for life and family, and above all, a passion for his God. This was a man who had an intimate knowledge of Christ that was obvious to anyone who knew him. It was a deep friendship that had been cultivated for decades, a relationship with both warm sweetness and fiery zeal to do His will. To watch Mr. Walker conduct the choir was like watching a master craftsman molding an exquisite instrument, whether they were singing a centuries-old hymn or the most popular new worship song on the Christian charts. He did not merely direct the music, he brought it to life, embraced it, and offered it up to God as a sacrifice of love. From the first time she had heard the choir Liz had observed the affection and respect that every singer had for this man of God. It seemed the easiest thing in the world for him to direct them; it was as if every singer were an extension of the man himself.

Suddenly she felt the honor and privilege that was being offered to her, and she somehow knew that if she turned it down she would end up regretting it.

"OK," said Liz. "If you're doing it, I will, too."

Rehearsals were both interesting and satisfying. Mr. Walker made no allowances for newcomers but seemed to assume that they were experienced vocalists. This approach was both flattering and challenging. In writing about the experience in her journal, Liz could think of many words to describe rehearsals with Mr. Walker, but "boring" was never one of them. He always began with a few words to put their work into perspective; they were not *practicing* to worship God, they were worshipping Him, with every act, every repetition, every corrected mistake. He had instilled in every choir member, and soon had instilled in Liz, that every note one sings, even the off-key ones, could be an act of worship, if one's heart belonged to Jesus. Moreover, *every* act or deed—changing a tire, washing a dish, cleaning a toilet—could be worship, if offered up to God. (Liz tried to remember this whenever she didn't *feel* like doing her laundry.)

Although at the beginning there was much practice of separate parts, Mr. Walker made sure that every rehearsal contained at least one portion of the oratorio that was sung with the complete choir. The sound of the beautiful music coming together in its fullness was inspiring and left each choir member excited and looking forward to meeting again.

Liz particularly loved "For Unto Us a Child Is Born," one she had heard sung in her church in St. Louis. It always brought back the feelings of Christmas past, and whenever she sang the words "And His Name shall be called: Wonderful Counselor..." her heart glowed with the warmth of a wonderful secret, known only to a select few: that she had first met Christ through a dream, where He was her Advisor, Confidant, and Best Friend. To hear a full choir sing such apt praises of the One she knew so intimately brought her chills and made her feel somehow connected across the centuries to the composer himself.

George Friederich Handel. Charles Walker. What a privilege to sing in the company of such giants in the faith!

CHAPTER TWENTY-ONE

As they pulled into the driveway in front of the modest ranch house, Liz felt a butterfly or two. Although she had seen Mrs. Walker among the other choir members and sung under the direction of Mr. Walker, she had not had an opportunity to speak more than a greeting to either one of them. She was a little nervous about meeting these two who seemed to be major celebrities in the church. She pulled down the visor to check in the mirror for any hair or makeup blunders.

"I hope they like me!" she whispered as she flipped it back up.

"What's not to like?" he whispered back loudly. "Just get the mascara off your nose and you'll be fine." Liz whipped the visor back down.

"Psych," Sean laughed. She smacked him on the arm. "C'mon," he said. "Let's go."

As they traipsed through the crisp, colorful leaves that blanketed the yard, a huge golden retriever came bounding around the corner to greet them just as Beverly opened the door.

"Ludwig! No!" She grabbed him by the collar just in time to keep him from knocking Liz down. "What an overgrown baby!" she scolded, shaking her head apologetically at the two guests. Come on in, kids. Chuck, you wanna take the greeter?" she said looking over her shoulder at her husband who had also appeared in the doorway. Mr. Walker took the dog from her. "Why don't you put him in his pen out back?" Beverly suggested.

"Come on, fella," he said to the wagging bundle of gold, and with some difficulty he led him into the kitchen and out the back door.

Beverly sighed, smiling at Liz and Sean. She greeted them with a warm hug that dissolved any apprehensiveness Liz might have felt. The house had a homey, festive smell; the aromas of roast beef and rolls combined with spicy scented candles and potpourri.

"Have a seat, make yourselves comfortable," said Beverly, gesturing to two armchairs as she sat on the sofa. The décor of the living room was traditional yet colorful; the Walkers apparently liked purples and blues. As Liz sank into the deliciously comfortable chair, she looked around at framed pictures of family members that were lovingly displayed on walls and shelves amid sculptures and arrangements of silk flowers. Speakers placed discreetly behind potted plants softly played a Chopin nocturne.

"What a beautiful home you have!" Liz exclaimed. Just then she spotted a grand piano in the bay window, elegant looking in spite of the cascading sheets of music that were strewn on, under, and around it. Beverly spotted it, too.

"Chuck?!" she called in a voice that meant business.

"Yes, dear?" said the master of the house, who was just coming in from penning up the "child."

"I thought you were gonna do something about this mess!" she scolded. Liz noticed Beverly had a hint of a Southern accent, which came through only in moments of "exasperation," though it was plain to see the woman didn't have an angry bone in her body.

Mr. Walker strode over to the piano defiantly and began rooting through the papers until he found what he was looking for: a small plaque reading, "Creative genius is seldom tidy." He placed it in a prominent position among the stacks, where all could read its words of wisdom. Satisfied that he had "done something about the mess," he joined his wife on the sofa.

"Liz, what're we gonna do with these men?" Beverly asked. The Southern accent was still there, but her eyes twinkled. Liz stifled a laugh.

"Dinner smells delicious!" Sean exclaimed, effectively changing the subject.

"Don't let it fool you," Mr. Walker replied, poker-faced. This time Liz couldn't suppress a giggle. "Can I get you something to drink? Coke? Ginger ale?"

"Coke's fine for me," said Sean.

"I'll take ginger ale," said Liz.

The conversation before dinner revolved around the Walkers' family, prompted by the many pictures in the room. Liz learned that the Walkers had a daughter in Ohio married to a minister, who played the organ in a small church and kept busy raising two small boys and a baby girl. The Walkers also had a son who was a high school music teacher in Springfield who had a special love for the *Messiah*, as his father had.

"Jeff was so excited when I told him we were doing the whole thing," said Mr. Walker. "He's been practicing the tenor parts on his own so he can join us as soon as school gets out. Just think!" he exclaimed excitedly. "The *Messiah!* The debut of the new church! Christmas Eve! It will be like a glimpse of heaven!"

"Tell her the story about Handel when he was writing the *Halleluiah Chorus!*" Sean requested.

"You haven't heard it?" Mr. Walker asked Liz.

"I don't think I have," said Liz, trying to think back to her classes in music history. But by the look on Mr. Walker's face she could tell that it was a story he had told numerous times without growing tired of it, and she felt sure that even if she had heard it before, she would enjoy hearing it again, especially from him. Mr. Walker reminded her of her best professors at the university, those who were passionately interested in what they taught and had the gift of making others interested, even passionate, too.

"Handel wrote the *Messiah*—the whole thing—in just a few weeks' time…"

"You're kidding!" Liz exclaimed.

"Not at all," Mr. Walker replied. "It was one of those divinely inspired creations. Not that God isn't in other endeavors, the kind requiring hard, even tedious work. But this was one of those times the work itself seemed to be the driving force." Mr. Walker's eyes shone, and the excitement in his voice grew. It was clear that he had experienced similar bursts of inspiration himself.

"Handel had locked himself in his room for days without seeing anyone. He wanted to be left alone, and the servants left his meals outside the door. Sometimes they would come back and the food would be untouched. Finally someone in the household became so concerned that he knocked on the door to make sure the composer was all right. He had been writing the *Halleluiah Chorus,* and according to the servant, his face 'shone like that of an angel!'" As he said this, Mr. Walker himself had the look of one who had seen beyond the mundane things of the world. "Handel declared that he had 'seen heaven open up and the great God seated on the throne!'"

"Wow…" Liz murmured.

"And that's what we're gonna sing!" Sean added with more than a hint of excitement in his own voice.

"Yes!" Mr. Walker declared, practically rising out of his seat. "I've dreamed of doing this … oh, *forever,* ever since I was in school."

"And we won't talk about how long ago *that* was!" Beverly added with a wink.

From the kitchen a buzzer sounded.

"There goes the smoke alarm. Dinner must be ready," Mr. Walker quipped. Beverly looked at Liz, sighed, and shook her head.

"Come on into the dining room, kids," she said to all three of them. "Dinner'll be on in a minute."

The dining room was small with a simple elegance about it. French doors led out to a brick patio overrun with ivy, and the drapes hung about the window in a unique artistic design. The plain white cloth on the table was accented with blue cloth napkins. Two blue candles were set on either side of a modest centerpiece of flowers from the garden. Beverly had Liz set the basket of rolls on the table and light the candles as she brought in the roast.

"Chuck, would you toss the salad please?"

"Sure, honey, where would you like me to toss it?"

"Sean, would you toss the salad please?" The dialogue sounded almost rehearsed, and Liz got the feeling this was a regular part of the Walkers' entertaining, or perhaps a ritual left over from their days with a house full of children.

When everything was on the table, Mr. Walker reached out a hand on either side as Beverly did the same, and Liz found herself in a circle of four, joined together in prayer. It was as if Liz had always known them. They gave thanks not only for the food, but for their lives, for love and friendship, for the presence of a loving God so strongly felt in that room.

"How long have you known Jesus, Liz?" Mr. Walker asked when they had finished dinner and retired to the living room with their coffee. The question was one Liz had heard before, but she had not yet come up with a simple answer for it.

"Well, I'm not sure. It's kind of a long story."

"We'd love to hear it," said Beverly. "Would you mind telling us?"

If anyone else had asked, Liz might have felt she was being interrogated, but Beverly and her husband both seemed genuinely interested and looking forward to a good story. They never tired of hearing about people's discovering their Lord. As for Sean, she didn't want to bore him with telling the story again, but he seemed anxious for the Walkers to hear it.

"Yes, tell them about it!" he encouraged her.

"Well, I was raised in a church, so I was familiar with it all—the Bible stories, the hymns, etc. But about nine months ago I had this dream … I dream a lot." She watched their faces, afraid they might think she was a bit strange, but they showed no disapproval, so she continued.

"In the dream I met this person at school. He seemed to be someone I had seen around a lot but had never gotten to know, although I think that was just in the dream, because I haven't seen anyone like that since." The Walkers seemed to understand, so she went on.

"He was a grad student, studying psychology to be a counselor, and I sorta got the feeling he was studying me. He was so kind, so easy to talk to, although he didn't talk much—not nearly as much as I did. I remember that what he did say was so wise, so profound … although I can't remember anything specific now," she added.

"Dreams are so often like that, aren't they?" said Beverly understandingly.

"Anyway, there was something else about him that I didn't quite understand. He was handicapped. I guess now we're supposed to say 'special needs.' He was legally blind and had cerebral palsy. Yet he could see other things, things most seeing people can't. It was like he was seeing into my soul. He was such a good friend, and he meant so much to me. I even told him I would marry him, and it seemed so right … Then I woke up.

"I couldn't believe it had been a dream. It seemed so real, and he still seemed like my best friend. I didn't really have many friends then. The only people I saw regularly were in the theater department, and I didn't really feel like I fit in there. But I couldn't shake this feeling that this person *did* exist, and I couldn't forget him. For a while I even tried to find him, but there was no such student on campus, at least not as far as I could see." Liz paused, remembering the frustration of those days.

"It must have been a lonely time for you," said Beverly sympathetically. She and her husband were holding hands, their fingers entwined as they listened.

"It was. It's funny. I had just landed a pretty big part in a musical at school, and it was what I had really wanted for such a long time, but I wasn't even happy about it. It seemed empty. All I could think about was the friend I had lost, although I kept trying to shove him out of my conscious mind. It just hurt too much to think about him, and I didn't even know who he was. I just had one hint: his name began with a 'J.' In the dream I had called him 'J' for short, though I didn't know what the 'J' stood for." Mr. Walker followed what she was saying with a look of knowing.

"And how did you find out it was Jesus?" he asked. It seemed ironic to Liz that "J's" identity was so clear to him when she had struggled for so long to figure it out.

"Well, I was with my parents at church. I was home on Easter break. And the sermon was kinda dull, I don't even remember what he was preaching about. I picked up what I thought was a hymnal, to sort of leaf through it, but I had accidentally picked up a Bible. On the other hand, I guess with God there are no accidents…" The Walkers exchanged glances, smiling as though sharing a special memory, and Beverly gave Liz a wink but didn't interrupt.

"When I opened it, it was right at Isaiah 53, and the words seemed to jump out at me—all the pain, the rejection from people that my friend had experienced, and that he had 'born our griefs and carried our sorrows.' It was just like this friend; he had listened to all my troubles and complaints and had eased my pain just by being there and understanding. But I still didn't know who it was that Isaiah was describing, and the minister was too busy to explain it to me. I guess he might have if he had known how important it was to me to know."

"So you still didn't know it was Jesus?"

"No. They didn't talk much about prophecy at our church, at least I don't remember their mentioning it. I knew enough to know that the Old Testament was stuff *before* Jesus, so in a way it may have actually kept me from figuring it out sooner. Seeing this description in Isaiah just kind of intensified the desire to know. And I guess it pointed me in a 'God' direction. I finally prayed and asked the Lord to please show me what it all meant, or else help me to forget about him, so I could get on with my life. But that hurt, too—the thought of forgetting him—because in spite of my frustration, I didn't want to just forget him, he had become too important to me.

"Then I had another dream. This time he wasn't crippled or blind. He stood up straight, looked at me with … these eyes …and was calling me to come and be with him forever. I knew it was Jesus, because when He reached for me I saw these big gaping wounds in His hands. And I knew He wanted me to make a serious lifetime commitment to Him, because in the dream … I was wearing a wedding gown."

"And you said 'yes'?!" said Beverly eagerly; she had tears in her eyes.

"I did."

"Excellent!" exclaimed Mr. Walker, scarcely able to contain himself. "So you first knew the Lord as your Wonderful Counselor," he mused. "That explains it."

"Explains what?" Liz wondered.

"The look on your face when we practiced *For Unto Us a Child Is Born* yesterday. When we got to the 'Wonderful Counselor' part, your face was radiant. You were thinking about your relationship with Him, weren't you?"

"Yeah, I guess I was," Liz admitted. "I didn't realize it showed."

"The eyes are the windows to the soul," said Beverly. "Whatever is inside us will come out sooner or later. If it's not in your words, it'll show on your face." Her own face was radiant.

"What a gift you have!" exclaimed Mr. Walker.

"Gift?"

"Yes! To dream dreams from God."

"But everyone has dreams…don't they?" said Liz.

"But not many remember their dreams much, and fewer really know how to interpret them, like Daniel, Joseph—both Josephs. Other cultures have put great stock in dreams as revelations from God. Of course, we have Scripture for that, and one wouldn't try to pry meaning out of every little dream that comes along. But when they confirm Scripture, when they are this profound and *God* shows you the meaning, it is a special gift He wants you to use."

"Use how?" asked Liz, intrigued by the idea.

"Young lady, you have vision." The authority in Mr. Walkers voice made Liz sit up and take notice. It was quite a change from the host who had earlier penned up the dog and stuck a plaque on his musical mess. "You see things in a different way than others do. We each know God from our own perspective, and we need to *share* these perspectives so we can *all* know Him *better*. You say you dream frequently, and I would guess you dream in color," he added. It was a statement, not a question, and he didn't wait for her to confirm it. "You have a creative mind. God will use that. You like to write?" This time he waited for her to confirm his assumption.

Liz almost laughed at this point as she exchanged glances with Sean.

"Actually, at this point I feel that's what the Lord is calling me to do."

"Excellent!" Mr. Walker exclaimed again. "Listen to God and *do it!* When He tells you something—big or small—write it down!" The man's face shone, confirming what Sean had told her about Mr. Walker from the very beginning, that he was a man of great passion and inspiration. She had been hesitant to visit this couple, who were held up in such high esteem by the church, thinking somehow they would make her feel so small. Yet here they were, encouraging her to be all she could be, and more.

Just the way "J" used to do.

"So, how do you like the Walkers?" Sean asked on the way home, though he knew full well the answer.

"I *love* them!" Liz exclaimed. "They are such wonderful, encouraging people! You and everyone else had made such a big deal about them, I thought I'd feel dumb and small around them, but they didn't make me feel inferior at all."

"*Truly* godly people are like that," Sean observed. "It's usually the baby Christians that try to intimidate people, to try to make themselves look holier than everybody else. The Walkers aren't like that. If anyone feels guilty around them, it's the Holy Spirit doing it, not them. They just love people, because they love Jesus."

"Well, *I* love *them,*" Liz stated decisively. "I'd love to be one of their children or grandchildren."

"Well, I'm sure they'd love to adopt you," Sean laughed. "I could tell they like you, too."

CHAPTER TWENTY-TWO

The call came at 1:15 AM. Awakened from a deep sleep, Liz fumbled for the phone, knocking her clock radio onto the floor. She immediately recognized Sean's voice and was wide awake at once when she heard what he had to say.

"Pray for Mr. Walker, Liz. There's been an accident."

"What?!" she gasped.

"After we left their house he and Beverly took Ludwig for a walk. While they were on their way home he was hit by a drunk driver." Liz clapped her hand over her mouth.

"Oh no!" she cried. "Where is he?"

"Cook County Hospital, intensive care."

"But what...? How badly...?" she stammered.

"They don't know yet. The car struck him in the back, and when he hit the pavement... Closed head injury, possibly brain damage. There seems to be some paralysis. Right now they're just hoping he'll make it through the night. Just *pray*, OK?"

"OK," said Liz in a voice that was barely audible. There was a pause as she waited for Sean to say something more, more news, an encouraging word, anything. But all he said was,

"Look, I gotta go call the rest of the prayer team..."

"OK, I'll talk to you in the morning," Liz replied, choking on her tears.

She hung up the phone in a daze, then buried her face in her pillow.

"Oh, Jesus! Not Mr. Walker! Please don't take him..." She thought of the logic of praying for someone *not* to go to heaven. "I mean, not yet! O Lord, this was his dream, to do the *Messiah* for You—Christmas Eve, in the new sanctuary! Please let him do it! It would bless so many people, it would glorify You so much..." And she went on for the next hour or more, praying as though the Almighty needed to have everything explained to Him, begging, reasoning, bribing, until she came to the end of herself, and her soul, exhausted, collapsed into submission.

"'Nevertheless, not my will, but Thine be done,'"[1] she quoted half-heartedly, then cried herself back to sleep.

Rehearsals went on, with the assistant director in charge, but they were more like prayer meetings than practices. Everyone was praying for Mr. Walker, and everyone, it seemed, had a different opinion of what God was going to do. The age-old controversy of faith and healing grew. Being a non-denominational church, Faith Chapel had persons of many religious backgrounds—or no religious background at all. Some prayed with childlike simplicity that God would just touch and heal Mr. Walker; some secretly worried that if God didn't heal him immediately, such childlike faith would evaporate like a morning mist, and then what would such tender believers do? Some tried to explain that God always answers prayer, but sometimes the answer is "yes," sometimes "no," sometimes "wait." This was not much comfort, and some, frustrated to the brink of tears, questioned, why pray at all then?

Some prayed for wisdom for the doctors and for healing to come through them. Others prayed that the Lord would bypass the medical profession completely and so glorify Himself only. Some prayed for God's perfect will, not merely His permissive will; others wondered what in the world that was supposed to mean. Some even prayed "warfare prayers," using voices full of authority, quoting the Bible as though waving a sword, and telling the devil in no uncertain terms that he could *not* have Chuck Walker! Others not only prayed for healing, they *claimed* it, quoting Scriptures that God would prove true, and becoming annoyed to no end with those who insisted on adding "...if it be Thy will" at the end of their prayers. *Of course* it was God's will—He said so, right there!

Relatively inexperienced believers felt intimidated by those who could quote a staggering number of Scripture verses; however, the latter were outdone by the ones who professed to know what the words meant in the original Hebrew, Greek, and Aramaic and volunteered to interpret for everyone.

"But we don't really *know* what Paul's 'thorn in the flesh' was," one member of the group protested, while another added,

"What about Job? He was a righteous man, and God let him suffer for a time..."

"*Satan* tormented him, not God," yet another joined in the debate.

"But he had to get *permission* from God to do it!"

"And he got permission!"

"Exactly! He *petitioned* God. That's why we have to *counter-petition…*"

As Liz tried to sort out what "counter-petition" meant, someone else changed the subject.

"Did you know that the word in Revelation for 'witchcraft' is 'pharmacea?' We get the word 'pharmacy' from it."

"Meaning…?"

"It means literally *'communing with the devil* through the use of *drugs.'*"

"Are you saying…?"

"I don't trust doctors!"

"We need to stop talking about paralysis and brain damage. We need to say 'he's whole!'"

"Isn't that lying?"

"No! He's actually already healed. The Word says 'by His stripes we were healed.'[2] The symptoms are the 'messenger of Satan.' *Satan's* the liar! Chuck just needs to stand on the Word of God!"

"So you're saying that Chuck's problem is he just doesn't know the Bible well enough and needs to have more faith?"

"Well, the Word does say…"

"That godly man!? That's the most ridiculous thing I've ever heard!"

There was even talk of some alternative treatments, which was met with righteous indignation that anyone would suggest the use of a New Age method, which everyone knew was from the pit of hell.

A few tempers flared, and some days it seemed certain people had nothing in common except their concern for Mr. Walker.

His wife Beverly bore it all patiently. At first she did not show up at rehearsals, and everyone knew she was at her husband's side, no doubt comforting him with her encouraging words and sweetness of spirit. Later she would come in and seem awkwardly self-conscious, not wanting to create a distraction. Everyone knew that so much wanted to be said, yet very little was, verbally. Still, there was the touch of a hand, a gentle smile, a hug that said so much, and Beverly accepted with tearful gratitude every expression of support.

For Liz, there was the impatience that came from praying everything she could think of to pray, and praying it again and again, until she thought surely the Lord must be sick of the whole thing, and why didn't He just heal Mr. Walker and get it over with, so we can get on with the *Messiah?* Then, with the realization that she was *not* God and could do nothing more, her soul settled into a kind of numbness.

There was much rejoicing when four weeks later Mr. Walker showed up for rehearsal. He was in a wheelchair and looking pale and haggard, but his spirit shone through. And though some members boldly insisted that "God's not finished yet!" he was deeply grateful for the use of his arms, and declared that, God willing, he would be conducting the *Messiah* on Christmas Eve. This announcement brought a standing ovation, whether for Mr. Walker, God, or both, and among the sopranos there were a few tears shed.

He proceeded to carry on the rehearsal as though he'd never been away, and soon Liz could see the fire in his eyes as he led them in Handel's magnificent tribute to his God. She could imagine the composer smiling to see such dedication and oneness with his music. There were moments when it seemed the director would rise right out of the wheelchair—indeed, everyone hoped that he would—yet the conducting continued from the humble position of the paraplegic, and to Liz, the chair seemed to mock his name.

Rehearsals with full orchestra began in mid-December, and the choir was treated to the solos that had been practiced separately up to that point. Undoubtedly Beverly's was the most moving. Although she had a score in front of her, she never so much as glanced at the notes; likewise, her husband conducted by heart, sometimes with eyes closed in near ecstasy, other times looking deeply and passionately into his wife's eyes as she sang:

"I know that my Redeemer liveth..."

Their faces reflected the peace of undaunted faith. To watch and listen to this couple was an inspiration. One could sense the many years they had spent growing together in trust and knowledge of God, and that they fully expected to continue doing so right into eternity.

I hope Sean and I will be like them someday, Liz thought.

When Beverly finished her solo, the silence that followed was profound. Every soul in the room had been elevated to a higher level. Such is the effect of true faith on those around it.

Almost equally moving was Gordon Mayfield's singing of *Comfort Ye My People.* The young man had an excellent, well-trained voice, and of course the solo exuded peace, a rare commodity as the Christmas season approached with all the secular distractions the world had created to pollute it; with the added stress of the recent accident, a moment of serenity was a welcome relief.

It was during the second rehearsal after Mr. Walker had returned that Liz was enjoying Gordon's singing with her eyes closed and a peaceful smile on her face.

Suddenly she was startled out of her reverie by the sound of a collective gasp from the other choir members. Gordon stopped singing, and Liz opened her eyes to see a disturbing sight.

Mr. Walker was slumped back in his chair, his body shaking convulsively, his eyes rolling back in his head. Dr. Peterson had already leapt off the platform and ordered for someone to call 911. Beverly flew to her husband's side, musicians began moving their instruments to clear a space, and most of the choir sat in shocked silence. Liz felt as though she were going to be sick.

The next few moments were a blur; Dr. Peterson's orders were mingled with Beverly's soothing words of encouragement, others' prayers, sobs, and eventually the wail of sirens. In spite of the rapid technical dialogue between the doctor and the paramedics, everything seemed to be moving in slow motion until Mr. Walker was finally taken away, with Beverly and a few close friends following. As the flashing lights of the ambulance flickered through the windows and the siren's melancholy cry faded into the night, Liz dreaded the heated controversy that she expected to follow.

But there was no theological debate, no arguing, no proud declarations. There were prayers, and there were tears, and people who recently had barely spoken to one another now sat quietly, nonjudgmental, heads bowed and hands clasped in unity. Beside the cluster of music stands, a group of musicians stood in a huddle, arms around one another, and one was softly leading in a prayer. A few others pretended to busy themselves with cleaning and putting away their instruments, but Liz noticed the awkward looks on their faces. These were people she did not recognize; they were not members of the church, but professional musicians that had been hired to fill in the gaps. Liz couldn't help wondering what was going on in their minds. Did they know the Lord at all? If not, what opinions were they forming about how He took care of His own? She found that she herself was unsure what she believed, and sitting in the midst of the emotional chaos, she suddenly felt confused and vulnerable. Looking down, she fidgeted with the pages of the musical score that lay in her lap. One large tear splashed onto the cover.

A moment later, she felt a strong, warm hand on her shoulder, and a familiar voice gently asked: "You OK, Liz?"

"... I'm not sure ..." she stammered in a choked voice, not looking up. Sean knelt beside her chair, lifted her chin, and looked into her eyes.

"He's going to be OK ... either way. We know that, don't we?"

Liz nodded, then gratefully accepted her fiancé's embrace and sobbed on his shoulder.

For the next few days the prayer chain kept the phone lines busy, keeping one another updated on Mr. Walker's progress. After just two days in the hospital, he was sent home with medication to control the seizures. Although there were those who believed that "perfect healing" was on its way and that medication was an unnecessary distraction, they had the decency not to be too vocal in their opinions, and most were grateful for any kind of answer to their prayers.

It looked as though Mr. Walker would be conducting the Christmas Eve service after all.

CHAPTER TWENTY-THREE

On December 23, the youth group gathered in the new sanctuary in their work clothes, amid stepladders, strings of lights, piles of garlands, and massive rolls of velvet ribbon. For the next few hours, the church reverberated with laughter, chatter, and boom boxes that alternated between Christmas carols and "contemporary" music that caused the floorboards to vibrate with the beat. The youth transformed the newly built sanctuary into a Christmas spectacle that was festive without being frivolous. Liz was struck by how enormous the place was and tried to imagine it filled with people.

"Do you really think it'll be a full house tomorrow night?" she asked Sean as she rolled up the remainder of the ribbon. Sean was sweeping pine needles into a dustpan.

"I wouldn't be at all surprised," he replied. "We get over a thousand people every week anyway, and it's been well publicized."

"True," said Liz. How well she remembered the stacks of posters they had run off in the office, and seeing them all over town the next day; the youth had done their job admirably. They had been sure to post the announcements in the music departments of the local colleges and universities, so that not only the faithful but also classical music enthusiasts would know about the concert. She felt an excitement similar to what she had felt before the musical production of *The Sound of Music* at the U. of I., when she had played a major role. Yet there was a difference this time. It was less fear, more thrill. Liz had no solos, no dances, no spotlight on herself to anticipate, yet she was no less excited. It was more the feeling of being enormously privileged to be a part—even a small part—of something so magnificent. When the curtain had gone down on the last performance of *The Sound of Music,* it had been over and done with, leaving an empty space of sorts in her heart and life. But this—this was timeless, eternal, and who could tell? There could very well be eternal results. God could bring anyone through that door, and who could hear the *Messiah* without being moved in one way or another, especially with someone like Mr. Walker at the helm? Liz felt like a child again, knowing that Christmas Eve would bring wondrous gifts, and though not knowing what they would be, brimming with anticipation.

Christmas Eve, an hour before the service was to start, the choir and orchestra members assembled in the choir room. The soloists were walking about in separate corners, doing vocal warm-ups. A few women still had random curlers in their hair. The chatter was low in volume, high in excitement. But all noise died down altogether when Beverly appeared with her husband. There was a reverent hush throughout the room as she wheeled him down the aisle to the front of the room, and all members of the company gravitated toward them.

Mr. Walker gazed affectionately over the gathering with moist eyes that had the look of one seeing beyond this world into another dimension. For a moment he said nothing. Then he began.

"Thank you. Thank you all for coming. As you know, this is the fulfillment of a lifelong dream of mine, to perform the complete *Messiah*. And you have helped make it possible—this magnificent work, dedicated to a magnificent God," (His face fairly glowed.) "with such people," he added, smiling appreciatively. "Every one of you has a gift from God—is a gift from God." For an instant his eyes met those of Liz, the youngest and newest member of the choir. "*Every* one of you. Don't ever forget that." He winked, and Liz felt as though she had been personally commended by a king. Was it wrong to feel pride at such a moment?

Mr. Walker's voice grew a little stronger as he went on addressing the company.

"I want you to know how much I appreciate your kind words, your concern, the help you've given my wife..." He reached up and patted her hand; Beverly never took her eyes off her husband as he spoke. "And most of all, your prayers. Prayer is so *important,* even if we don't know *how* or *what* to pray... and so often we don't. It's not so much what we say, prayer is in the *heart*. Prayer changes us. It may or may not change the situation, but it changes *us*. It's letting *God* be God."

He paused, then went on, softly yet passionately, "*Let God be God!* He has blessed us—blessed *me*—so much...

"If I had only my salvation, I'd be a blessed man, but He's given me more, so much more. A dear wife and soul mate ..." He squeezed Beverly's hand, and her eyes glowed with love. "... beautiful children and grandchildren who love Him and are here tonight.

And now..." (His face broke into a broad smile.) "... the fulfillment of a dream. If I die tonight, I would still be of all men most blessed."

Liz was troubled by this last statement. She wished he wouldn't talk that way! But Mr. Walker and his wife both had a look about them that was not of this world, and they seemed untouched by fear or trouble.

"We don't know what the future holds," Mr. Walker added with a confident smile, "but we know *Who holds the future.* I never would have guessed two months ago, out walking with my wife ..." His voice trailed off, and a few choir members awkwardly looked at the floor.

He took a deep breath and added with finality, "But let God be God. 'All things work together for good for them that love God.'[1] So love God, and let Him be God. He knows best. If I live another fifty years, if I die tonight, I'm a blessed man." He looked up into the face of his wife, who smiled back with the same serene joy. *"I'm a blessed man,"* he whispered fervently, his eyes gazing into hers.

The sights and sounds of the sanctuary were exciting and new, yet somehow familiar to Liz: the noise of the growing crowd, the butterflies in the stomach, the impatience to get started. Sean had been right in predicting a packed house; with the believers who had come to worship, the music lovers who had come to hear Handel, and the curious who had come to see the new sanctuary, it was obvious that every seat would be taken. The excited conversation, blended with the orchestra's tuning up, gave an air of expectancy. In the dim light a myriad of candles flickered. The smell of wax mingled with that of fresh pine and perfume. Spruced-up youth, some in their fathers' suits and ties, stood at each doorway, giving out programs, searching the balcony for empty seats, and asking parties if they could please move down to make room for a few more.

As the choir came in single file and began filling the platform, voices were hushed and house lights faded. Orchestra members ceased their warm-ups, and a few audience members cleared their throats. Beverly wheeled her husband to the music stand at the front, and a low murmur rippled through the crowd. As she positioned the wheelchair, something seemed to make her hesitate. For a moment the two of them looked into each others eyes, smiling as if to say, "We made it!" There was visible love between them that was almost enviable, in spite of the obvious troubles they had been through.

Before taking her place with the choir, Beverly kissed her husband, and though it wasn't a long, drawn-out kiss, it seemed somehow sacred, like the culmination of a wedding ceremony. Liz felt a twinge of fear. Was she kissing him good-bye?

From the first note, there was something about the way Mr. Walker conducted that night that was different. The fire and passion was still there, and he seemed to be drinking in every moment as though savoring a rare delicacy. This was to be expected, of course. Everyone involved felt the same way; how much more the one for whom it had been a life-long dream?

Yet there was something else about him that Liz noted, and she wondered whether anyone else could see it. Mr. Walker seemed to know something that the others didn't, and Liz didn't want to think about what that might be.

Gordon's *Comfort Ye My People* was more exquisite than ever, and though half the choir held its breath, nothing went awry this time.

For Unto Us a Child Is Born was for Liz like finding the door of heaven ajar and peering in.

"And His Name shall be called … Wonderful … Counselor …
The Mighty God, the Everlasting Father, the Prince of Peace!"

She felt that she had sprouted wings and could take off at any moment. Mr. Walker's face reflected the same ecstasy; his eyes seemed to behold unspoken wonders, and at times they had an unexplained intensity.

When Beverly sang *I Know That My Redeemer Liveth,* there was a profound sense of peace and sacredness that was felt by every soul in the place. Liz marveled that Beverly could continue to sing with such a steady, clear voice; she knew that had she herself been the one singing, she would have been blubbering through most of it.

A few songs later, Liz felt a thrill rush through her as she realized the *Hallelujah Chorus* was next. This was the part where the composer had seen " all of Heaven…and the great God!" She had no doubt that it was possible for that entire congregation of thousands—believer and unbeliever alike—to gaze upon God's face if He willed it. And why wouldn't He?

She was almost too breathless to sing when the orchestra began the famous melody, and the mass of people stood to their feet according to the royal tradition. It seemed cruelly ironic that the only one *not* standing was the one for whom it meant the most.

The choir had never sounded so magnificent; they were singing their hearts out for *their* Messiah, and for Mr. Walker. They were giving him his Christmas gift, and one could tell by his face that it was the finest he had ever received.

"HA—LLE-LU-JAH! HA—LLE-LU-JAH!
Hallelujah! Hallelujah! Halle–lu-jah!"

The words echoed like a blessing on the new sanctuary and everyone in it.

"For the Lord God Omnipotent reigneth!"

The words seemed to echo Mr. Walker's words: *"Let God be God!"* And the "hallelujah's" that followed thundered through the hall, the kettledrums booming for emphasis. The intensity in Mr. Walker's face increased, and he conducted as though fighting some kind of battle that raged within him; Liz couldn't tell if he was winning or losing. When they sang

"And He shall reign forever and ever!"

there was look of victory on his face, and the words *"Let God be God!"* echoed in her heart. Liz was so busy watching Mr. Walker's expressions that she nearly forgot to turn the pages of her score, and she found it difficult to keep up.

Mr. Walker didn't have to try to keep up; he didn't need a score. This music was in his blood, and he pursued it relentlessly, with a look of fervent determination on his face.

As the song built to its climax, there was suddenly something different about his expression. It had a wide-eyed quality about it, a look of acute surprise that seemed to be overwhelming him. Liz couldn't tell if it was a good surprise or a bad one, and that frightened her, especially considering the man's words to his singers earlier.

"King of kings!—Forever and ever!
And Lord of lords!—Hallelujah! Hallelujah!"
("Let God be God!")
"And He shall reign forever and ever!"
("If I die tonight, I'm a blessed man.")

No! Liz cried in her heart, even as she sang **"Hallelujah! Hallelujah!"** *Lord, You can't take him now! Please! Not now!*

"King of kings! And Lord of lords!"
("Let God be God.")
"King of Kings! And Lord of lords!"
("If I die tonight...")
No, Jesus! Please!
"And He shall reign forever and ever!"
("If I die tonight, let God be God.")

Liz was singing as if Mr. Walker's life depended upon it, and it seemed the rest of the choir was doing the same. As the final "hallelujah's" rang out, Liz saw to her horror that Mr. Walker was starting to shake again. His eyes had a look of utter disbelief, and as the choir stopped for the dramatic pause before the final "hallelujah," that pause seemed like an eternity in which the words echoed, *If I die tonight, let God be God.*

The choir was holding its collective breath, waiting for the signal for the closing line, and the audience appeared to be doing the same. Then something happened that was totally unexpected.

Mr. Walker's trembling hands suddenly grasped the armrests as if to steady himself and stop the shaking, and slowly, with a look of intense determination ...

He stood up.

Then still with a look of complete incredulity, he raised his arms in triumph.

Two miracles occurred that night. The first was that Mr. Walker stood before his choir, completely healed. The second was that somehow in their state of shock the choir still managed to sing the final *"HALLE—LU–JAH!"* as he directed them.

Since the whole audience was standing, most were unaware at first of what they were witnessing, except those in the first few rows and those in the balcony. Members of the church who knew Mr. Walker's story were awestruck. Strangers were puzzled, and a few cynics thought it was in poor taste for such a prominent church to resort to such a corny publicity stunt.

Beverly, of course, knew better. She stood reverently as the applause thundered, tears glistening on her cheeks. Her husband was gazing beyond the audience, oblivious to the ovation.

Ordinarily at that point the orchestra, choir, and soloists would each take a turn at accepting the applause, but somehow individual bows seemed out of place that night. The only One worthy of praise was receiving it all.

No one wanted to go home that night. Why would anyone who had tasted heaven want to return to earth? Liz, of course, responded to the night's happenings the way she responded to any profound event in her life; she cried profusely. Sean wrapped his arms around her and shook his head in affectionate amusement, but his eyes were glistening, too. All around there were tears and hugs, and one of Mr. Walker's grandchildren expressed the feelings of most as she jumped up and down with glee, clapping her chubby hands and squealing with delight. Seeing her, "Grampa Chuck" crouched down and opened his arms wide. The toddler ran to him and was lifted, giggling, into the air. "Gramma Bebberly" looked on, her face beaming with pleasure.

The following day, Christmas Day, the church received word that Charles Walker had gone to be with his Lord, sometime after midnight Christmas Eve. He had slipped away quietly in his sleep, leaving this life the same way in which he had walked it, with a look of profound joy on his face.

CHAPTER TWENTY-FOUR

In a sense everyone had been right, and everyone had been wrong. God had proven beyond a doubt that He was perfectly capable of performing a miracle of healing any time He chose. And the time He had chosen had been one when many, many witnesses could experience a glimpse of His glory that they could not deny, and that they would never forget.

At the same time, He had also made it very clear that *He* was in charge of the lives of His people. If He wanted a man to live, that man would live until his work was complete. If He wanted to call that man home, no one could keep him in this world— nor should anyone want to. *"Let God be God"* was to become the unofficial motto of the choir, if not the whole church.

God had also proven that there were worse things than physical problems, and there were better things than instant healing. During the Walkers' tribulations, the church had undergone a transformation. Whereas before there had been no lack of opinions (and opinionated persons to express them), there were now honest questions and open minds. More importantly, there were open hearts.

Mr. Walker had told the youth group once that when he was a teenager he had had all the answers, but had somehow grown more ignorant since then. Recognizing his wisdom, the teens had realized that sometimes it's better to have sincere questions than too many answers, and that God is much more concerned with a person's character and relationship with Him than he is concerned that a person get everything "right." Even if such a thing were possible, "getting it all right" would inevitably lead to pride and self-sufficiency, the first stage in the downfall of a church.

And so, in the months following Mr. Walker's accident, Faith Chapel had become a place where there were many more questions than answers, but where the questions did not seem to bother people as much as they had before. There was the peace of trusting that a loving God knew everything, and that if and when they needed an answer, it would be there for them. Meanwhile, the questions and mysteries were marvelous opportunities to exercise faith. And of course, in the Christian life faith is what it was all about.

Thus Faith Chapel, in spite of its tremendous success and every human reason to become arrogant, was actually a kinder, more compassionate church, one in which members bore one another's burdens and differences of opinion with patience and love enough to puzzle any outside observer. What was even more puzzling was the fact that most people had very little awareness of the change that had taken place. Maybe it was because they were embarrassed and reluctant to think about past destructive attitudes that had been so hurtful to the cause of Christ, or maybe it was because they were too busy planning a bright future to analyze what had happened in the recent past. Or maybe it was that they were simply too close to the situation and it took someone from the outside such as Liz to see that the real miracle was not what had happened to Mr. Walker but what had happened to the church. Liz wrote in her journal about it in the quiet moments that brought such insights, but she shared these thoughts only with Sean, who marveled with her at the new attitudes they were witnessing. In such a large group of extremely diverse personalities, attitudes like these were nothing short of a miracle.

And the miracles continued. Beverly Walker had requested a memorial service for her husband on what would have been his sixty-fifth birthday. Since the date fell close to Easter that year, it seemed especially fitting that the service included an encore solo from the *Messiah, The Trumpet Shall Sound.* Cliff Johnson was more than willing to sing in Charles Walker's honor, but there was doubt as to whether the trumpet player the church had hired would be willing and available to return for the service.

Providentially, he was free that day, and actually excited to take part in such a tribute.

As a multitude of family, friends, and admirers listened, Cliff sang:

"The trumpet shall sound ... and the dead shall be raised,
Be raised incorruptible..."

A joyous atmosphere of victory filled the place. Everyone felt it, and as the trumpet player accompanied triumphantly, one could see in his expression a passion reminiscent of Mr. Walker's.

After numerous testimonials regarding Mr. Walker's character and his influence in people's lives, the pastor wrapped up the service by asking if there was anyone who had postponed a relationship with Christ, for whatever reason, and invited these procrastinators to make a commitment then and there to the Lord that Mr. Walker had loved so. Several came forward and knelt at the front, and to everyone's delight, these included the trumpet player. In an outpouring typical of the emotion of an artist, he laid his trumpet on the altar, signifying his commitment to dedicate his music to glorifying God.

From then on the instrument was seen every Sunday at the church, where the musician—Charles Walker's last convert—played it faithfully every week in the worship. His name was Randy Simpson, and in time he became like another son to Beverly.

CHAPTER TWENTY-FIVE

"Let this be written for a future generation,
That a people not yet created may praise the Lord."
—*Psalm 102:18*

The dream lasted only a moment, but it was one that Liz would always remember.

As the vision was fading and the morning light awakened her fully, she lingered in bed, etching the picture into her memory. She smiled as a wave of peace swept over her.

"Thank You, Jesus," she whispered.

"I think I've seen Mr. Walker," she told Sean over their customary cup of coffee in the church café.

"Really? You dreamt about him last night?"

"Well, actually, this morning, right before I woke up. It was just for a few seconds, but I saw it so clearly. Two men were standing together. Their backs were to me, but I'm sure one of them was Mr. Walker. The other was dressed very differently, like from another century, and he had lots of hair. It may have even been a wig…"

"Handel?!"

"I don't think I ever knew what he looked like, but that was my first thought."

"What were they doing?"

"They just had their arms around each other's shoulders, as though they'd been best friends all their lives. They were talking. I couldn't make out what they were saying, but they seemed to be speaking almost simultaneously, finishing each other's sentences, that sort of thing—real kindred spirits. I heard them laugh. Then I woke up."

Liz could tell by the look in Sean's eyes that he had caught the vision.

"Sweet…" he sighed.

"Yeah, what a blessing. I can't wait to tell Beverly about it."

"Yeah, she'll like that," Sean agreed. There was a pause during which Liz felt a certain lack of satisfaction, almost frustration.

"I just *wish* I could do *more*," she said, her voice beginning to break. "Oh Sean, I was just getting to know him, and now he's gone!" A tear rolled down her cheek. Sean reached across the table and squeezed her hand.

"Y'know, Liz, the best thing you can do to pay tribute to Mr. Walker is to use your gift the way he encouraged you to do."

"You mean write?"

"Yes! As he said, you're a visionary…"

"—an eye in the Body of Christ?"

"If you wanna put it that way, yeah. I mean, think about it, Liz. You look at a special needs student and see the Wonderful Counselor. You look out the window of an airplane and see a mission field. You look at a contest and see battles raging everywhere.—You see angels on the subway!" he laughed. "And while the church is watching for God to heal an injured believer, you're watching Him heal the *Church*. As Mr. Walker said, 'write it down!'"

Liz smiled wistfully. "Sarah once told me that, too."

"Then I guess you'd better do it," Sean announced with an air of finality.

"Sean, you know how scatterbrained I am." Sean didn't argue with her.

"Mm-hm."

"And a procrastinator…"

"Yep."

"So you remind me and nag me, OK?"

"I'll nag like I've never nagged before," he promised.

So from that day on, whenever Liz had a revelation, a dream, an adventure, or an answered prayer, as soon as she had finished telling Sean about it, he would rejoice with her; then he would repeat the familiar admonition—"Now *write it down*." And she would … usually.

Of course, things to write *about* far outnumbered the opportunities to write, and Liz soon realized what the apostle John meant when he wrote, "Jesus did many other things as well. If every one of them were written down, I suppose that even the whole world would not have room for the books that would be written." [1]

Liz imagined herself in her old age, when all the adventures had died down, writing and writing about what she had seen the Lord do in her lifetime; she hoped her memory would be good enough to do so. If it wasn't, or if the adventures never died down (a definite possibility), she'd wait until she got to heaven and tell these stories for all eternity to anyone who wanted to hear.

EPILOGUE

"Hello?" Sean's face lit up when he heard the voice on the other end of the line. "Uncle Phil! How are ya? How's everything in the Big Apple?"

"Busy, as always. How's my favorite nephew?"

"Couldn't be better."

"I figured as much. Hey, I got your invitation. I can't believe little Shahnee's getting hitched!"

"Yeah, it had to happen sometime…"

"Seems like the last time I saw you, you were all dressed up for some goofball grade school play."

"First of all, it was high school, not grade school," Sean corrected, pretending to be offended. "And it wasn't some goofball play, it was *The Pirates of Penzance!*"

"Well, believe me, seeing my little nephew swinging from the yardarm looked pretty goofball to me," Uncle Phil chuckled.

"Yeah, I can sorta see that it would," Sean admitted. "So, are ya coming to the wedding?"

"Oh Sean, I really want to, but I can't. I won't even be in the country until the day after. It's our annual Big Deal in Tokyo, and ever since I got that promotion they're expecting me to be a part of it. Gotta earn that pay raise, I guess."

"Bummer! I was really hoping you could come, but hey, did you say you'd be back home by Sunday?"

"Yeah, Sunday night. Why?"

"Well, because…" Sean paused for a dramatic effect. "Liz and I are coming to New York for our honeymoon! Maybe we could get together sometime that week."

"You're *what?!*" Uncle Phil demanded with mock outrage. "Sean O'Brien, with all the exotic places to go for a honeymoon, what kind of people go to New York?"

"Theater people! We're gonna take in the sights and go to a *ton* of Broadway shows! Besides, believe it or not, Liz has *been* to all the exotic places, but she's never been to New York except to change planes. Can you believe it? So instead of exotic, we're going for *glamorous.*"

"Well, if you're going to 'see the sights,' you've *got* to see the Twin Towers, and you'll need a tour guide."

"Still pretty proud of yourself for working there, huh, Uncle Phil?"

"Hey, what can I say? I like the view."

"So, how about it? Can we get together?"

"Sure, that'd be great. Monday I'll probably be pretty swamped catching up from the trip, but how about Tuesday? We can have breakfast at Windows on the World, and I'll show you around."

"Windows on the World?"

"At the very top of the North Tower. You can look out over all of Manhattan."

"Sounds great. I'll give you a call that Monday night. Uncle Phil, you're gonna love Liz. She's the greatest."

"She'd better be, for my favorite nephew! Hey, I've gotta go, I've got a call on my other line, but I'll see you two in a couple of months."

"Can't wait! See ya then!"

"'Bye, Shahnee."

"It sounds like our honeymoon's already being planned," Liz observed when Sean had hung up the phone.

"Yeah, my favorite uncle lives in New York, and he actually works at the World Trade Center. You thought the Sears Tower was something, wait'll you see that place! Uncle Phil said he'd show us around. You're gonna love him, Liz! He works for a huge corporation, but he's in sales and marketing, so he's got a lot of the 'performer' in him, too. He's funny, full of stories, real fun to be with."

"So when are we going to see him?"

"That Tuesday…" Sean looked at the calendar. "September eleventh."

To Be Continued…

SCRIPTURE REFERENCES

Chapter One
[1]I Corinthians 12:4-6
[2]I Corinthians 12:12
[3]I Corinthians 12:14-20
[4]I Corinthians 12:21
[5]I Corinthians 12:22
[6]I Corinthians 12:24b-26
[7]I Corinthians 12:27
[8]Proverbs 29:18 (KJV)

Chapter Four
[1]Matthew 11:30
[2]John 16:33
[3]Isaiah 6:1
[4]Isaiah 53:3
[5]Isaiah 6:2, 3
[6]Isaiah 6:4
[7]Isaiah 6:5-7
[8]Isaiah 6:8
[9]Isaiah 6:8

Chapter Eight
[1]Psalm 8:4

Chapter Fifteen
[1]Psalm 23:1
[2]Psalm 23:4

Chapter Twenty-Two
[1]Luke 22:42 (KJV)
[2]I Peter 2:24

Chapter Twenty-Three
[1]Romans 8:28 (KJV)

Chapter Twenty-Five
[1]John 21:25 (NIV)

Books by Ann Aschauer

Awakening Series
Book One: *Counselor*
Book Two: *Vision*
Book Three: *Sparrows*, Release Date: 2011

Available through Isaac Publishing, Inc.
http://www.isaacpublishing.com
1.888.273.4JOY

Also available through other popular online book retailers.

To contact the author:
BAscha3870@yahoo.com